*

Pepin County is in the grip of an icy winter; twenty degrees below zero as the new year rolls in. Deputy Sheriff Claire Watkins is happy. She's been living with Rich Haggard, and as they sit together awaiting midnight, she feels ready to step into the marriage he's wanted all along.

But not all marriages last. Car mogul Daniel Walker is celebrating New Year's Eve alone, roasting in his sauna with a bottle of Belvedere vodka by his side. His soon-to-be-ex-wife Sherri has left him at their cabin, and he's glad to be starting fresh. What better way to symbolize his new freedom than by a quick roll in the pure white snow? Daniel braces himself for the cold and, naked, heads outside.

He's found the next morning, frozen and covered in snow.

Claire must investigate Daniel Walker's family and friends as doctors pump warm fluids into his body, struggling to thaw and revive him. Meanwhile, the new year brings new life to Pepin County as a local teen gives birth to an unexpected child.

In the chill of midwinter, Claire discovers that every warm body has the potential to house a very cold heart ...

The Claire Watkins Mystery Series

Blood Country

Dark Coulee

Glare Ice

Bone Harvest

Poison Heart

Maiden Rock

Point No Point

FROZEN STIFF

FROZEN STIFF

A CLAIRE WATKINS MYSTERY

MARY LOGUE

TYRUS
BOOKS

Published by
TYRUS BOOKS
1213 N. Sherman Ave. #306
Madison, WI 53704
www.tyrusbooks.com

Library of Congress Cataloging-In-Publication Data has been applied for

12 11 10 09 08 1 2 3 4 5 6 7 8 9 10

978-1-935562-11-5 (hardcover)
978-1-935562-10-8 (paperback)

In the infinite winter of space,

heat is tiny;

it is the cold that is huge.

—PETER STARK, *Last Breath*

to Alison and Ben, for persevering

NEW YEAR'S EVE

11:55 pm

Even though it was twenty below zero outside, wind blowing up a storm, Daniel Walker was stark naked and sweating like a boxer in the beyond balmy two hundred degrees of his cabin's new sauna.

This is the life, especially in the dead of winter, Walker thought as he tilted his head back and blew smoke from his Davidoff double corona up toward the cedar ceiling. The cigar wrapping was wet and unraveling, but he was almost done. A bottle of Belvedere vodka, nestled in a rapidly melting block of ice, sat on the wooden bench next to him. Wynton Marsalis was blowing his horn through the Bose speakers.

All was so calm. Taking a large swallow of vodka, he could feel the liquid easing its way into his stomach, then sliding into his veins while the sweat beaded up all over his naked body.

Toxins in, toxins out.

Slowly he poured another shot of vodka down his throat, enjoying the feeling of the freezing drink cooling his insides. He had much to celebrate—a terrific new land deal that was going to save his ass, even as his car dealership was struggling. And he was pretty sure he was going to be able to step out of his marriage without giving Sherri a penny, bless his pre-nup.

In the end, he would probably throw her a bone, just to make up for any hard feelings. She wasn't a bad sort, but he had grown tired of her.

Dan wouldn't have minded some sweet young thing in her birthday suit sitting next to him, ready to massage any part of his anatomy that required it, but women did bring problems no matter how careful you were. Much as he loved them. He tried not to think about his latest fiasco.

He wondered what his darling daughter Danielle was up to tonight. She certainly took after him. She enjoyed partying as much as anyone he knew. Too busy to come out and see her old dad. But you were only young once.

Yesterday, he had texted her an invitation to join him in the sauna for the new year, but she had texted back: "Big Pop, no way. Hanging with bffs." That was his kid!

Glancing up at the clock in the sauna, he saw it was nearly midnight. Perfect timing. He was so hot he thought his liver was going to melt. He banged through the sauna door, took a gulp of the cooler air in the ground floor basement. Not cool enough.

Dan braced himself, then pushed open the back door and stepped outside. When the frigid air hit his naked skin it burned hotter than the sauna.

Glorious. Looking down from the edge of the bluff, he couldn't see a house from his place to Lake Pepin. The snow glittered like the exterior of a new white car and the air smelled almost as good.

After taking a couple long strides, Dan threw himself into a snow drift. His skin pulsed hard and deep all over his body. He rolled over on his back and looked up at the pattern of pinprick stars. Who needed anything more than this? His breath rose up in plumes. He was his own Mt. Vesuvius.

Dan felt like he could lay there all night, staring at the stars until they fell into his brain. Moments passed as he slowly felt the warmth ease out of his body. No worry. The sauna would heat him back up.

His skin stung as if it had been scrubbed with a hard brush. Pins and needles all over. He crawled to his knees, then stood up and spread his arms wide.

Happy New Year to me!

The wind was picking up, blowing the snow into him, which felt like BBs hitting his skin. His feet were freezing and he could feel the warmth of his core leaving him. Time to get back into the sauna to warm up before he headed off to bed.

Dan hopped on his stiffening feet to the door and, shivering, pushed down the latch. Nothing happened. Must be stuck. He pressed it down harder, but it wouldn't budge. Then he slammed his shoulder into the door, but no movement.

Why wouldn't the door open? He couldn't have locked it. He didn't have the key.

All he could think was that it had somehow gotten jammed.

Stepping back, he thought of running around the house, but remembered that he had already locked the front door for the night.

Dan shivered hard—fear and cold cracking down on him. He had to get into the house. The cold was searing his skin. He slammed his whole body against the door, but it wouldn't open.

Break a window, that's what he needed to do. He pounded on the picture window by the back door, but his hands were worthless. They just bounced off the glass. Damn those custom windows he had special ordered for the ground floor. Unbreakable, they claimed.

Squatting down, he tried digging into the snow to find a rock, a branch, anything, but he was getting so cold. He was shaking so hard he could hardly think. His whole naked body was racked with convulsions.

Finally his hand hit a piece of cement left over from a project last summer. He lifted it in both his hands and walked up to the window, hoisting it over his head, he slammed it into the window.

The chunk of cement bounced back and hit him square in the face. He stepped back and tried to keep his balance.

Dan looked back toward the door and saw a form in the window. He tried to remain standing but his head ached and his legs gave out. His eyes rolled back as he fell.

Blowing snow covered him like a blanket.

CHAPTER 1

I'm ready, thought Claire as she watched the fire pulse deep red in the woodstove, *I want this for the rest of my life.*

She was reading a bird book Rich had bought her for Christmas. He was nodding off in the chair next to her, his head bent over and the book in his hands about to fall. The stroke of midnight had come and gone. They had clinked their glasses and finished off the bottle of champagne and then, too comfortable to get up from their chairs, decided they would watch the fire for a while longer.

Claire couldn't believe they had made it past midnight. They hadn't managed to stay up so late the last few years. She tried to convince herself that she wasn't waiting up for Meg to come home. Her daughter had gone to some friend's house to play her new Wii game, and had promised she'd be home by one. Only one time had she not made her curfew, with disastrous results. But since then, she had been Johnny-on-the-spot.

Hard to think that in less than two years, Meg would be gone. She was slowly pulling out of their lives already, working at the Red Wing YMCA on Saturdays and taking a college class in River Falls, driving an old Toyota Corolla that Rich had fixed up for her. Claire found it hard to imagine life without her energetic, darling daughter breezing through it.

For eight years she and Meg had been living with Rich in his family farmhouse, longer than she had lived with her husband. Rich reminded her of the Mississippi, which flowed just a block away from where they were sitting: down the driveway, across Highway 35, and through the Fort St. Antoine park. He moved along steadily, but those waters ran deep and, every once in a while, he would surprise her in an amazing way. He was her able companion and had been next to her, supporting her through some very hard times.

Claire knew that he had trouble with how involved she got in her work. Being the lead investigator—the only investigator—for the Pepin County Sheriff's department did put a crimp in her home life from time to time. Rich would complain, and then have a good meal waiting for her when she finally showed up.

For all his griping, Rich more than supported her. He had grown up in Pepin County, unlike her, and he understood how vital her police work was to the health of the community. He knew how information moved through the county, he knew who was related to whom, he knew the lay of the land. He was her guide in what had been a new country for her and often told her what she could not see.

He was a good man and the love of her life.

Claire turned to wake him. The book was wavering in his lap. When it fell, Rich jolted awake. Claire laughed.

He glanced over at her to see what had happened and then smiled with warmth in his eyes.

"Time for bed?" she asked.

"I guess."

She rose from her chair and knelt down next to him. A touch of gray showed in his black hair. She reached up and brushed his face. "Will you marry me?"

He shook his head as if to clear it, then said, "I don't know. I kinda like it the way it is."

She swatted at him with her hand. He pulled her up into his lap and took her face in his hands. The kiss wasn't like the hungry embraces they had at the beginning of their relationship, it was deeper and more satisfying. A kiss that said I'm here, next to you, where I will always be.

Claire heard the back door open. Rich and she pulled apart as if they had been caught doing something they shouldn't. Then they laughed. Her daughter was home. She heard Meg open the refrigerator door, always her first act when she walked into the house. Like most teenagers, she was constantly hungry.

"Hey, old fogies! You stayed up." Meg came to the doorway of the living room and yelled in her outdoor voice, "Happy New Year!"

New Year's Day: 3 am

The woman lounged in bed, waiting. She knew he would be here soon. She loved this time before he came, the anticipation of his energy, his desire. In many ways, her imagining what was to come was better than what actually happened. Her New Years's Eve would start when he walked through the door.

She had gone out with Carly and Petra for a few drinks at midnight, but when some guys starting hitting on them, she cut out. The girls were like, You can't leave now. But she knew those two could handle the men all by themselves.

The radio was playing party music. She had taken a long bath, done her nails, put on a silk t-shirt, then taken it off, and climbed into bed. She had thought of getting a bottle of champagne for the occasion but he was more of a Budweiser kind a guy. She had a six-pack waiting in the fridge.

While she lolled in bed, she imagined her life to come. Just travel for a while. Paris sounded good to her. Her French wasn't half shabby. She knew how to say, "Voulez-vous coucher avec moi ce soir?" As long as she could say that, order a glass of wine, and buy some clothes, she'd be set.

A knock sounded on the door of her apartment. Finally. She waited a minute. The next series of knocks came louder, harder.

She rolled out of bed and walked to the door, swishing her hair back over her shoulders.

She opened the door and watched his face open when he saw her standing there, naked.

"Whoa," the tall boy said.

She led him to the bed without saying a word. There would be time for talking later.

New Year's Day: 6 am

Clyde Hegstrom knew the cows didn't really care that he had been up late last night, way past his usual bedtime of nine o'clock, nearly closing the bar. He milked them at six in the morning because that's when they needed to be milked, their udders filling up to the point of pain otherwise.

His herd of six cows also didn't care that his 17-year-old daughter Bonnie had delivered a baby two nights ago, and almost lost her life doing it. That he had drunk himself silly last night. That his wife was so upset that she couldn't even talk. That she hadn't been home in two days. The cows didn't care that it was twenty below zero with windchill too low to measure.

Clyde could hear their soft lowing as he trudged to the barn. His head felt heavy on his neck and filled with compost.

The barn smelled of cud and sweet hay. The cows turned their heads to him and greeted him with loud snuffles and moans, all in their own familiar sounds. He didn't have to think about what to do. The pail came to his hands, the stool sat on the ground. He still milked his small herd the old-fashioned way. He was sure he got more milk out of them that way, and he was even more sure that they enjoyed it more.

He started with Hilda, the oldest cow, who was pushing eighteen, the upper end of her life span. Her mother had rejected her so Clyde had raised her with a bottle. She was his big baby.

He leaned his head into her warm, soft hide, his hands started their work, milk hissing down into the pail. The warmth of the cow's soft body comforted him and he found tears bathing his face.

New Year's Day: 9 am

Sherri Walker was not looking forward to going back to the "cabin" as Dan called it. She hadn't been there in a month, since Dan had dropped the divorce bomb on her as they were having drinks.

He had chucked her under the chin, like a little girl, which she hadn't been in thirty years, and said, "Don't think this marriage is working any more." She had started to cry, but tears never worked on him. The only thing that worked was sex and while he hadn't turned her down that night, he hadn't been overly enthusiastic. A week later, he had divorce papers served on her.

As she slid down the long, ice-rutted driveway in her blond Saab, the car Dan had given her for her birthday this last year, she figured he was probably nursing a nasty hangover. Any excuse for overdoing it.

She had decided, come what may, she was going to keep the car. As his gift to her, she didn't think Dan could take it away from her. But she knew she wasn't going to walk away from this marriage with much else. Plus, she didn't know how she was going to support herself since she had been out of the work force for five years. When they had married, Dan had insisted she quit her job, saying he didn't want to have her working for him anymore, or at least just in bed.

Her eyes prickled as she came into view of the house they had built during the flush of their first year together. Dan had wanted it to be a cabin so they had kept it under 4000 square feet. The structure sat on the edge of the bluffline slightly closer than was legal, depending on where you measured from. After the inspector had been there and signed off on it, Dan had moved the stakes. He was proud of that. He never liked anyone telling him what to do. Especially not her.

While the footprint was modest, the house soared three stories high: the master bedroom filled the whole top floor. The structure felt like a treehouse. Shingled in cedar, it had a green metal roof. She had insisted on that color so it would blend in to the treeline. Dan had let her have her way on that one decision. He must have loved her then.

Sherri wished she could hate Dan. She wished she could be really angry at him, but the person she was mad at was herself. What a fool she had been. When your boss takes you on a business trip and then buys you a sexy outfit while his wife doesn't even know you're with him, you have to know what you're getting into. How could she have ever thought he would change his ways?

Dan was what they called a *puer*. Sherri remembered this term from her college psychology class. A Jungian term, it described a man who never wanted to grow up: Peter Pan, Mick Jagger. Bill Clinton for that matter.

Sherri parked the car right by the front door. They had had a pretty civil conversation two nights ago. She had asked Dan if she could come to the cabin and get some things. She was staying in their house in town, but wanted a few of her sweaters and a book she had left out here.

The front door was locked. Sherri shook her head. Dan brought his city mentality with him. When she was staying alone at the cabin, she never locked the doors. But then she had grown up in a small town where no one ever locked anything.

She dug her key out of the bottom of her purse and unlocked the door. Stepping in the house, she could smell the faint whiff of cigars, one of Dan's many vices. The kitchen light was on and the house was very still. She had noticed how the snow blanketing everything also muffled sound. Dan must still be sleeping. She hoped to god he didn't have a visitor with him. Even he couldn't be that crass.

Kicking the snow off her boots, she hollered, "Anyone home?"

Maybe he wasn't there. Maybe he had gone off with someone last night. She decided not to bother taking her boots off. Dan still had the cleaning lady come in every other week. A dirty floor wasn't her problem anymore.

She walked through the house and looked into the garage. His car was there. His BMW with every option available. His one true love had always been the cars.

Cautiously she made her way upstairs. Not only was Dan not in the bed, but it wasn't even rumpled. She walked to the floor-to-ceiling windows and looked out at the lake. This view is what she would miss more than anything. The windows were west-facing and looked out over the treetops. The lake was covered with snow and shone like a vast expanse of glittering field, cupped in the hollow of the bluffs.

A red-tailed hawk flew out from the bluff and she went with it, soaring out over the lake. For Dan this view had meant power, for her it had meant freedom, a sense of the earth that she had never had before. She had learned all the birds, could even identify them by the way they held their wings as they glided.

Dan couldn't tell a chickadee from a bald eagle.

Sherri pulled out a carryall and went through her drawers, grabbing the few sweaters she wanted. Most of the clothes she had left in the cabin she didn't really care about.

Dan might be sleeping in the downstairs family room. Sometimes he fell asleep in front of the TV. As she walked down the two flights of stairs, she thought of leaving without even seeing him. They had little to say to each other anymore. But when she stepped into the bottom floor she felt how warm it was. He must have left the sauna on.

She didn't see him anyplace. The sixty-inch flat-screen TV was dark. The couch was empty. She pulled open the door to the sauna and a blast of hot air hit her in the face. A bottle of vodka sat on the bench in a pool of water, a sodden cigar butt next to it.

"Dan?" She turned off the heat in the sauna and checked the back door. It was locked, but she went to the window and looked out. Snow covered everything. She looked at her garden and could make out the clump of hostas from the flower stems still sticking up. But it looked like there was a good foot of snow.

Just as she was about to turn away, she saw an odd form, like a snow-covered log, in the middle of her flowerbed. A tree branch fallen down? A dead deer?

The lump was quite large, long. She couldn't remember anything being there this fall.

She stared out the picture window, then noticed it was smeared with handprints. Even though the cabin might not be her responsibility any more, the prints made her mad. How had they gotten there? What had Dan been up to?

The wind blew up large eddies of snow, twirling up like miniature tornadoes. As she watched, the snow drifted off the form in her garden, uncovering some of it. She still couldn't tell what it was. From this distance, it looked like a hand, but how could that be?

Without thinking, she moved her head forward until her nose bumped the window. She was sure she was looking at a hand. She could make out the glint of a ring. With horror crawling up her throat, she tried to make what she was seeing something else—a dried flower, a pale stone, a piece of statuary. But the ring looked like Daniel's signet ring. How was that possible?

If that was Dan's hand that meant he was buried in the snow. Could he have been so drunk last night that he had fallen down in the snowbank and not been able to get up? What had happened to him?

She had to get to him.

Sherri reached down to open the door and found it locked. The dead bolt was in place. How could it be locked? Dan couldn't have locked it when he was outside unless he had a key.

Her hand shook as she tried to undo the bolt. She had to get to him. She had to get him help.

The bitter cold knocked her in the chest. She ran out into the snow, then stopped and stared down at what she could now clearly see was a waxy hand, like that of a mummy, no color to it.

She sank down in the snow and touched the hand, then wiped clear his face. He had turned to ice.

He must have been locked out and then froze to death. No one deserved that. Not even her bastard husband Dan.

In some part of her mind, she knew he was dead, but the thought that he might still be alive pushed her to call for help.

CHAPTER 2

Amy unplugged the block heater on the squad car, climbed into the frigid vehicle, and turned the key. Sluggishly, the car engine turned over, but didn't catch. She slapped her mittened hands together, waited a few seconds, then tried again. She didn't want to wear the battery out. This cold weather had gone on for too long. What she wouldn't give for an attached garage, but she guessed she was lucky that an off-street parking place came with her apartment.

With relief, she heard the engine come to life, gave it a little gas, turned the heat on full blast, and then climbed back out to clear all the windows. The ice was especially thick on the front window. After she scraped it all off, she saw there was even some ice on the inside of the car.

Seeing that the heat gauge needle had risen, she backed up and got on the street. No one else around. She only lived about six blocks away from the government center, easy walking distance, except on a day like today. Could freeze your face off in less time than it took to tie up a horse.

When Amy walked into the sheriff's department, she caught Tanya yawning at the front desk, a party hat tilted on her red hair like the leaning Tower of Pisa.

"You look ready to go home," Amy said.

"Got that right."

"Busy night?" Amy asked.

"Not really. I've lived through worse New Year's Eves. I think the snow and cold kept the partying to a minimum. Two drunks are sleeping it off in the jail and a kid wandered away from a party, but Bill found him sleeping in the barn, visiting with the cows."

Amy was glad to hear that Bill had worked last night. Even though they hadn't been seeing each other for a while, she still kept track of him and hated to think of him having fun without her. Right after she broke up with him, he had been mad for a few days, then he ignored her for a couple weeks. Now they were almost back to being friends, casual friends, but at least he would say hi to her. She knew it wasn't very nice of her, but she wanted to be the first one to start seeing someone else.

"Roxie coming in?" Amy asked.

"She called to say she'd be late," Tanya lifted up her party hat, then let it snap back down. "I just want to climb in bed and sleep until tomorrow. I guess it's called hibernating."

"Anything going on this morning?"

"Yeah, we got a call from near Stockholm, something about a dog."

"I'm going to drive down that way. They had a break-in down at the Short Stop a couple days ago and I want to check back with them."

"Perfect. On your way you can check out the Walker residence. A woman called and said that there was something in her backyard. She didn't call on the emergency line so I don't think there's any big rush."

"Sure. Did she say what?"

"She seemed pretty calm about it. I think she said her dog. I couldn't hear her that well. She kept breaking up. I think she was calling on a cell phone."

"Why's she calling us about her dog? She should have called animal control. Last thing I want to deal with this morning is a dead dog."

"Why don't you swing by—it's on your way."

At least the car was still warm, Amy thought as she climbed back into the vehicle, a cup of steaming coffee balanced in her hand. She drove down 25 waiting for the sun to crest Twin Bluffs. These bitter cold days were always bright, clear, and often still. Absolutely beautiful. Right as she approached highway 35 the sun lifted up over the bluffs, sundogs on either side of it. She pulled into the wayside stop there, a convenient spot to tuck in and catch speeders, drank her coffee and stared at the two lines of rainbow, frost glinting in the milky sunlight.

Ten miles down the road, she turned the car up the bluff. The plow had already been through and the road was slippery, but cleared.

The Walker house rose over the crest of the driveway, an odd tower of a house, all the lights on in the early morning dawn, the sun barely topping the field. Amy was always amazed at these houses that lined the bluff, like masters of another race come to live among the peons for a while.

A gorgeous fawn-colored Saab sat in the driveway, its tracks the only sign that marred the new snow. Amy parked the squad car behind it and got out. Still below zero, breathing in the cold air made her cough. Before she had even taken a step the front door was flung open and a blond-haired woman stuck her head out.

"Thank god, you're here. I can't get him out of the snow." The woman was crying and her hands were red.

Amy knew how hard it could be to lose a pet. She walked up the front step. "Let's see what you have here."

The woman was shivering, her skin was pale and her lips were turning white. Amy could tell she was going into shock. "Let's get you in the house. You need to put a coat on."

The woman babbled, "I didn't know what to do. I tried to uncover him, but it's so cold. I think he's frozen stiff."

"What kind of dog is it?"

The woman looked at Amy in astonishment and said, "It's no dog. He's my husband."

New Year's Day: 10 am

Since he was old enough to sit at the kitchen table, he could remember this same red and white gingham tablecloth covering it. John Gordon sat in the kitchen, watching his 80-year-old mother pouring him a cup of her weak coffee, running his finger on the checkerboard pattern.

He couldn't quite imagine a world without his mother—Edna Wheeler Gordon. Not that they had always been close, but no matter how far he had gone, spun out from her, she had always seemed the center of the universe.

His father had died when he was ten; he was killed when a tractor tipped over on him. After the funeral John's mother had told him that he had to be the man of the house. His sister Beth had only been five, too young to help out much. Together, he and his mother had run the farm for over twenty years.

If only he hadn't taken that job in Oklahoma this fall, but they had needed the money. Farming wasn't what it used to be and, in the winter months, he often needed to supplement their income. He should have known that his mother wasn't up to being on her own anymore. But he had asked Beth to keep a close eye on her and had thought that would be all the help she needed.

He watched Edna move slowly back across the kitchen floor and set the old coffeemaker down on the stove. Her knee was bothering her again, but she insisted she didn't want that blasted surgery.

"Why bother fixing something that I hardly use anymore? I'm not going to be around much longer," she'd say.

He hated to think of her alone in this house, but she was as stubborn as they come and she said the only way they'd get her out of here was to carry her feet first.

Edna walked back across the floor and sank into the chair across from him with a sigh, soft like air escaping from a pillow. Her body looked like a pillow, stuffed into the faded house dress she was wearing with an old sweater thrown over the top.

"Shit, you're still angry," she said.

"Mom, I'm not mad at you."

"I thought you'd be happy about it. I really did. I know I'm nothing but a burden to you and I thought this would take care of your problems." She turned her head down and her hands wrung themselves in her lap.

Edna had told him she wanted to surprise him. She thought that he would be happy that she had sold the farm and for such a tidy sum. But he knew it was only about half the going value of the place, 200 acres of land right on the bluff edge. Any developer would jump at the chance.

The fact that it was Dan Walker who bought it out from under him burned even more. Stupid schmo that he was, he had thought they were friends. John had spent the tail end of the summer building a sauna in the basement of that house Dan called a "cabin," and they had shared many a brewski. Dan's wife Sherri would stir up some dinner while he and Dan would smoke a cigar and look out at Lake Pepin. The view was almost as good as the one from the edge of his farmland.

Edna had signed away the land with the proviso that she be allowed to stay on in the farm until she died. Wouldn't be long now.

John looked up at his mother's face, weathered from years in the sun, tending the family garden, sometimes even driving the tractor. Her hair had gone completely white and her eyes shone bluer than ever.

He had been so mad when he came home for Christmas and learned what she had done. He had never yelled at his mother before, but he had not been able to contain himself.

Edna had been sitting in the kitchen, peeling potatoes. He had taken the cast-iron frying pan and thrown it against the wall, breaking her old blue vase. Looking up at her, he realized he should never have left her alone. Her brain was starting to muddle. He could tell, talking to her on the phone, that she was forgetting things and mixing up others.

When his mother died, the land that he had been born on and had sweated over for fifty years would be gone. He wasn't sure there was anything he could do about it, but he was going to try to get it back.

He held his mother's hand and whispered, "Sorry, so sorry."

CHAPTER 3
New Year's Day: 10:00

Claire couldn't believe what she was seeing. Amy had told her and she still hadn't been able to take it in. All the way on the drive over, she had wrestled with what she might find. Now she stared down at the frozen man curled into a fetal position—how we came into the world was the way we left it—one hand reaching out, fingers blistered, his skin waxy blue, his hair turned white with frost. The vulnerability of his pose made Claire's eyes water. Or the cold.

Only once before had Claire seen a man frozen to death. That had been during the coldest winter she had lived through, 1996. In February, when the temperature had dropped to 30 below with a windchill of minus 50, the governor had closed the state. No one was to go any place, except for cops. She had been on regular patrol and taken the call.

A neighbor, taking garbage out, had found the old man curled up against a wall in the alley. At least he had been wearing a coat. Somehow that made him seem not quite as vulnerable.

Remembering her lessons on hypothermia, Claire bent down, took off a glove, and put her fingers on Daniel Walker's neck. If there was a pulse there, it was too low and slow for her to tell. But it was still possible that there was life in this man.

She knew that people could survive in a deep freeze for hours, even days. The cold would have shut down his metabolism. The lungs would need less oxygen and the heart would pump less frequently. As the brain cooled off, it needed less oxygen to survive. Cardiologists even used chilling to get a patient ready for heart surgery, her pharmacist sister Bridget had told her.

So Claire knelt down in the snow and placed her head on his bare chest. She thought she heard something. A tick. A twig snapping. It might just be her own heart beating. She pushed in closer and listened again.

Yes, a slow, slight thud was coming from deep in the man's chest. A liquid thump which meant he lived.

She stood and yelled at Amy, "Get a blanket. We've got to get him inside. Call for an ambulance."

Claire took off her mittens, put her bare hands on his chest and rubbed in slow circles. Whatever life was left in him, she wanted to keep stoking. Maybe even just the warmth of human touch would keep him hanging on.

A minute later, Amy slammed out the door with a large down comforter filling her arms. "This was what I could find."

"Lay it out on the ground next to him. We have to move him very slowly. Any jarring at all will cause a heart attack. We don't want that."

They tucked the edge of the comforter under his body in the snow and then gently rolled him onto his other side, which moved most of his body onto the quilt. "Wrap it over him and then grab that end tight." Claire turned and yelled at Dan's wife, who was standing in the doorway. "Keep the door open. We're bringing him in."

Lifting him up in the comforter, they carried him slung between them. Claire backed up carefully as Amy directed her toward the door. "Slow and easy," she said as much to herself as to Amy.

Once through the door, they set him down on the floor.

"How about the sauna?" Amy suggested.

For a moment that sounded like a good idea to Claire, as much for herself as for the frozen man, but then she remembered more of what she knew about hypothermic victims. "That intense heat would be too much for him."

"We could turn it on low," the wife said.

"I'd rather not risk it. There's a weird phenomena known as rewarming shock. That's what a lot of people with hypothermia die from. They need to be rewarmed very slowly. Let's just keep the comforter on him."

"Is there anything we can do?" his wife asked as she sank to the floor next to Walker.

"Put your hands on his chest. Let him know you're there. Give him some of your warmth."

New Year's Day: 10:16 am

Meg ran her finger down the kitchen window, melting the hoarfrost that had gathered around the edges. She loved the patterns it formed, like miniature ice floes, like snow flowers. Whorls and twirls that shimmered in the pale sunlight.

"What's up with you today?"

Meg jumped. She hadn't heard Rich come in the room. "I don't know. Don't feel like doing much of anything. Too cold."

He had a million layers of clothes on, his fur-lined hat with the flaps hanging down, his leather-mitten choppers, a dirty down coat. The front of his dark hair had turned even grayer with frost from his breath. "The first day of the year and you don't know what you're going to do? Not a good start. Have you made any resolutions?"

"I might be swearing off boys."

Rich stripped down to his lined blue jeans and flannel shirt. He rubbed his hands together and grabbed the coffee pot. "Good idea. I highly recommend it. Are you going to make an exception for Curt?"

"No. He's the reason."

Rich sat down across from her at the table and poured himself a cup of coffee. "What's the problem?"

"Oh, nothing." Meg held out her cup and he filled it with coffee.

Rich stared out the window, cradling his coffee cup. "I'm worried about the septic. This damn cold. We don't have a lot of snow cover and the frost line could drop down far enough to freeze the lines."

Meg didn't really want to talk about their septic system. "Rich, are boys always jerks?"

Rich turned his head toward her and nodded. "Most of the time. Especially at that age."

"Curt's been hanging around with Andy Palmquist and he just seems different. All he wants to do is play those dumb games."

"What games?"

"You know, he's more interested in playing video games with Andy than watching a movie with me. I hate those violent, shoot 'em up games."

Rich took a sip of coffee. "That doesn't sound like Curt. From what I've heard, that Andy's a bad egg."

"I know. He gives me the creeps. He always looks like he's up to something. And he's always hanging around Curt. Like last night, I just wanted to go for a walk, with just Curt. Right at midnight, outside, the two of us. Something special. But he didn't want to. Said it was too cold."

"It was too cold."

"You know what I mean. Just for a few minutes. I didn't want to be with everyone else at midnight."

"Sometimes guys don't think like that."

"I guess."

"Let him know how you feel."

Meg remembered how it had been when she and Curt had started going out. He could read her mind. He always knew what she wanted. It had been kinda scary. "I don't want to have to tell him. He used to just know these things."

"He's not a mind reader."

"I want it to be like before, when we could sit and talk for hours. I don't feel like Curt has any time for me anymore. Like last night, all he wanted to do was play Wii with Andy. I mean, it's fun. I like doing it too, but not the whole night. Then when Andy takes off, it's like the night's over for Curt. He's bummed. Just wants to go home."

"Sometimes you can't leave it to chance. You have to be very clear with guys. Tell him what you want."

"I guess."

"Like your mom last night. She asked me to marry her."

"For real?" Meg squealed.

Rich gave his cute crooked smile and nodded.

Meg imagined her mother in a big white wedding dress. She would be beautiful. Meg could see herself in the perfect brides-maid's dress with Curt by her side. "When's the wedding? I've been waiting forever. It's about time."

"Not so fast. I told her I'd have to think about it."

"Not really. You're just teasing, right?"

"Hey, I've waited years. She can wait a few days for my an-swer."

Meg ran around the table and hugged Rich from behind. "Can I be your best girl?"

"You are my best girl."

New Year's Day: 11 am

Something shattered inside of Amy as she sat watching the EMTs carry a bundled Daniel Walker into the ambulance. Gary and Ted lifted the sling carrying the swaddled body gently into the back of the vehicle. What if Claire hadn't come to check out the scene? What if Amy had just left him buried in the snow, thinking he was dead?

"Gently, gently. I know you know this, but," Claire said, not wanting to step on any toes, "in cases of hypothermia, any-thing drastic can trigger cardiac arrest."

Amy stood by the front door and watched, thinking, I would have let him die. I didn't check him closely enough. I assumed. His death would have been all my fault. I might never even have known that he had still been alive. For some reason, that her mis-take might have gone unnoticed made it all the more horrific.

Claire came up next to her and said, "I'll take Sherri. I don't want her left alone, especially not in the house right now. We'll need to come back here no matter what happens."

"What do you think happened to him?"

"No way to know right now. We'll treat the house as a crime scene until we know otherwise."

Amy would have left him in the snow to die. She would have been responsible for his death. When she had watched Claire lean over the frozen man and put her head to his chest, she had held her breath, thinking, what if he were still alive? How could that even be possible?

Amy followed behind the ambulance as it screamed down the ice-covered roads, all she could think was what would have happened if Claire hadn't come.

I don't know enough, Amy thought. I think I've learned so much and then something like this happens and I realize I know so very little. Daniel Walker would have died if it had been left up to me.

CHAPTER 4

12:00 pm

Sherri watched as the doctor and the two EMTs slid Dan's stiff, contorted body onto a plastic mattress in the ICU. They had explained that it was filled with warm water that recirculated. As they started to attach electrodes to his body the doctor asked her to leave the room.

"But he's my husband."

An older nurse took her by the shoulders and walked her to the door. "We need to work on him and we don't need any extra people in the room. We'll come and talk to you in a few minutes."

The two women deputies were sitting right outside the door. They both looked up as Sherri walked out into the hallway.

"They're trying to warm him up," Sherri told them. "They said they have to start from the inside, then go out. They can't go too fast or he might die. What's going to happen?"

"We wait and see." Deputy Watkins told her. "It's a slow process."

Sherri sat down, but found it hard to stay sitting. She needed to call Danielle, but she wasn't looking forward to the conversation. As much as she had tried to like Danielle, to get the young woman to like her, they had never hit it off. She always had the feeling that Danielle was jealous of her. For the short time they had lived together, Sherri felt like the two of them were always vying for Dan's attention and affection. The situation had been quite unnerving.

"I'm going to step out and make a phone call," Sherri said. "I have to call Dan's daughter."

Amy stood up and said, "I'll go with you."

This comment startled Sherri, then she realized they didn't trust her. They felt they had to keep an eye on her. How could this get any worse?

"Fine." She didn't really care. She hadn't done anything wrong. When Dan revived, when he came back from the frozen depths, he would tell them that she hadn't even been at the house over New Year's. She didn't need to worry. If he came back from the dead.

She dug through her purse and pulled out her telephone book. It was a sign of how distant she and Danielle were that she hadn't even taken the time to program it into her cell phone.

The phone rang five times. Sherri was almost ready to hang up, not wanting to leave a message—what could she say—when it picked up.

"Hey," Danielle's sleepy voice said.

"Danielle, it's Sherri."

"Yeah, what's up?"

"Listen, I'm sorry to be calling you like this but it's your dad."

"What about my dad?" Danielle's voice sounded more awake. Then Sherri heard another voice, a male voice asking a question.

"There's been an accident," she might as well call it that until they knew more. It didn't sound as dire.

"With my dad? A car accident? What happened?" Danielle's voice was lifting up, growing thinner.

"I'm here at the hospital. It seems he got locked outside last night."

"What?"

"Yes, well, he was taking a sauna and he went outside to cool off I guess and the door locked and he couldn't get back in. He got hypothermia."

"What does that mean?"

Sherri tried to think of how best to put it. "His body temperature dropped and he got so cold that he went into a coma."

"You mean like he froze?"

"Yes. They're trying to warm him up right now."

"He's still alive?"

"Yes, but I think it would be good if you came to the hospital."

"Where? Where is he?"

"Durand. He's in good hands."

The phone clicked off and then the empty line buzzed in her ear.

Sherri leaned against the wall and cried. So like Danielle, she gets what she wants and then she hangs up. Even in this, her father in such a dreadful situation, Sherri would find no comfort from his daughter. If anything, the young woman would blame her somehow. Like Sherri should have been there, taking care of him. Then this wouldn't have happened.

Which was true.

New Year's Day: 1 pm

A soft voice whispered in his ear, "The baby's breathing on his own."

Clyde woke to find his wife Sara shaking him. He had fallen asleep sitting up in the hospital chair next to his daughter's bed. He hadn't heard his wife's voice in a couple days. What a relief.

"What?"

"They've taken him off the ventilator. He's breathing."

Being in the hospital always made him feel like he was swimming through water, everything moved at a different tempo, voices were muffled, the walls gave off an odd light. Clyde sat up and tried to come into the world. "That's great."

"I think he's going to make it. This little boy. Now if only Bonnie…"

"She will," he said, giving his wife the reassurance she needed, but he wasn't sure he really felt.

A few feet away, his daughter was lying still as a statue, white as a ghost. His lively daughter, who never stopped moving.

"I have to go home and then go to work for a few hours. You'll stay here?" It wasn't really a question.

"Are you sure you want to go to work? I don't think you need to. Anyone would understand."

She sighed. "I think I better." She looked over at her daughter. "We're going to need the money more than ever."

"Yes," he said. He knew he had to stay with his daughter even though it was the last place he wanted to be. Seeing Bonnie so absolutely still ripped him up.

"Call me. I'll have the cell. Call me if anything happens."

"Of course."

Sara leaned next to him and he could feel her shoulders shaking. She whispered, "Poor baby doesn't even have a name."

1:30 pm

Sitting on the hard chairs in the waiting room, Claire went over what she knew about what had happened to Daniel Walker. She thought back to what she had seen when she first got to the Walker's house—a naked man curled up in a ball out about five yards away from the house, his face uncovered and the side of his body blue in the cold air. The snow had been cleared away all around him, as if an animal had gone after him.

She turned to Amy, who was slumped into the chair next to her, and asked quietly, "Did you clear the snow away from him?"

Amy nodded toward Sherri who was sitting across from them in the waiting room, holding a magazine, but staring off into space. "By the time I got there, she had tried to dig him out."

"Why didn't she know he was locked out earlier?"

"From what I can gather, Sherri wasn't there last night. She claims she got to the house this morning and found him out in the snow, just like that, then she tried to get him out. She called the office, but somehow Tanya didn't realize what was going on, how serious this was."

"It looks like it was probably an accident," Claire said. "Poor guy wandered out into the snow after drinking too much?"

"Well, that's what's really weird. Sherri told me that the dead bolt was locked, which can only be done from the inside."

"Really?"

"That's what she said."

"Do you believe her?"

Amy glanced over at Sherri, then shrugged. "Why would she lie about that? Why not make us think it was an accident?"

"I don't know."

Claire looked over at Sherri, studying her. She guessed her to be in her late thirties, but very well kept up, all the latest products. Sherri was very dressed up for so early in the day. Claire could see smudges under her eyes, but other than that her make-up was perfect. A light blue cashmere sweater fit her to a T and white wool pants had a perfect crease down the front of each leg.

Claire walked over and sat down next to Sherri. "How're you doing?"

"I can't believe this is happening to me. It's just impossible. How could Dan let this happen?"

"What an awful thing to find. What do you think happened?"

Sherri shook her head. "I can't think. It's so unreal. When I got there I didn't know where he was."

"Why weren't you at the house last night? Where were you?"

"At our house in town. Dan and I, well, we're separated. I called him yesterday and said I wanted to come out to get a few things from the house. He knew I was coming. I hoped we would talk."

"Did you notice anything out of the ordinary when you first got there?"

"Not really. The house was so quiet, I wasn't even sure he was there. The bed hadn't been slept in. When I went downstairs, the sauna was still on. That scared me. Why would he have left it on? That wasn't like Dan. He was careful. Then I looked outside. At first he was completely covered with snow. Then the wind blew and…" Sherri's eyes grew larger, then filled with tears. "What if I wouldn't have seen him? What if he was still there?"

"You did see him. They're doing all they can for him." Claire decided to keep asking her questions. "So you think the back door was locked?"

"It was. The dead bolt. You can't lock it from the outside, only the inside. That's what I can't figure out. How could that have happened?"

"Do you think anyone was there last night with Dan?"

Sherri shrugged her shoulders, her hand dropped from her face. "Maybe. I don't know."

"Where were you last night?"

Sherri lifted her head up, her eyes wide. "At home. Alone. I went to bed early."

"Can anyone confirm that?"

"No. But that's where I was. I promise."

"Okay." Claire decided to let it go for the moment.

"Dan would have hated this." Sherri hung her head, her long golden hair falling over her face. Little rasping sounds jerked out of her mouth, and Claire realized Sherri was crying.

"Hated what?"

Sherri lifted her head, tossed her hair out of her face and swallowed, then said, "That someone could hate him enough to do this to him—lock him out in the cold. Daniel always wanted to believe that everybody loved him."

"Did they?"

Sherri finally looked at Claire, shook her head. "I don't think so."

"When you got to the house was it all locked up?"

"Yes. The front door was locked too. Dan always did that. He was a creature of habit, before this he had lived in the city all his life. He locked the door as soon as he was in the house, even when we were just hanging around."

"So all the doors were locked?"

"Yes, I already told you."

"Who has a key to your house?"

Sherri shut her eyes for a moment. "Let's see. We didn't have that many made. Dan, me and Danielle, his daughter. Then, our cleaning lady had a key. We were hardly ever there when she came. That's about it. I can't think of anyone else off hand. Dan or Danielle might have given one out to someone else. I don't know. I'll ask her when she gets here."

"Okay, let me know."

"Do you really think someone tried to kill Dan?" Sherri asked.

"I have no idea." Claire watched the woman. "What do you think?"

Sherri slid her eyes away from Claire's stare. "There doesn't seem to be any other explanation."

CHAPTER 5

New Year's day: 1:45 pm

His core temp was 80.5. Lowest I've ever seen." Dr. Elise Cornwall was standing over Claire in the waiting room.

Claire closed the *People* magazine she was reading. The news on Brad Pitt and Angelina Jolie could wait. "I didn't know it could go that low."

The doctor nodded. She looked like she was still a teenager, but Claire figured she must be at least in her mid-twenties. Dr. Cornwall had long blond hair, tied up high in a loose ponytail. She was wearing a lab coat with a cell phone sticking out the top pocket. Or maybe it was an iPod. She looked more like a soccer player than a doctor.

"But he's still alive?" Claire asked, looking around. Sherri and Amy had gone to the bathroom.

"Yes, remarkably. His temp actually dropped below 80 for a few minutes. Not unusual. It's called afterdrop, the residual cold pushes in on the core while the exterior of the body starts to warm. But his temp is on the rise now. We've been heating him up with intravenous fluid, but it's not enough." Dr. Cornwall looked around the room. "We're prepping him for surgery."

"What are you going to do?"

"We need to get more heat to his core. We're going to have to make a couple incisions in his abdominal cavity so we can set up a lavage of his internal organs with warm fluid. It's the only way we can get him warm enough, quickly enough."

Again, Claire checked to see if Daniel Walker's wife was anywhere close by, then asked, "What do you think? Is he going to make it?"

Dr. Cornwall flipped her ponytail, looking distressed that she would be asked such a blunt question. "I've never done this before. But I have to try something or we're going to lose him for sure."

Claire was also surprised by how forthcoming the doctor was with how dire the situation was. But Claire was often surprised at what people would tell a uniformed cop—they must feel comfortable speaking openly with such an authority figure, plus she was old enough to be the young doctor's mother.

"How long will it take?"

"Hours." With that comment, Dr. Cornwall turned and left.

A few minutes later, Amy and Sherri appeared. Claire filled them in on what the doctor had said, then watched Sherri sink into the chair next to her, her hand rising to her eyes. "It's going to be some time here, Amy. I'll stay here with Sherri. Why don't you go back over to the house and start checking around to see what you can see?"

"Do you want me to get anyone else over there to take photos?"

"Not yet. As long as we've got it secured. I'll stay with Sherri. I'd rather have just one person in the house at the moment. There'll be time soon enough to bring in the boys."

After Amy left, Claire turned to Sherri, "How're you doing?"

Sherri shook her head. "That sounds awful. Cutting him open. Do they have to do that? What does this mean? Did she tell you if he was going to make it?"

"Dr. Cornwall seemed to feel this was the best chance of bringing him back safely."

Claire didn't add, if anything could. It was not her job to squelch hope in the victim's family. But she couldn't help remembering the line she had once heard about persons suffering from hypothermia: "They're not dead until they're warm and dead."

2:30 pm

Meg lounged on her bed, listening to her music, drawing a picture of a snowflake. She liked playing with the patterns that they made, symmetrical. So you just had to figure out a fourth of it and then replicate it. A beautiful puzzle.

Her cell phone was resting on the bed next to her. No phone calls, no messages. Usually Curt checked in, even if it was about nothing. She hated being so aware of him, of how he was treating her. She wished she felt more sure of herself, that she didn't care so much about him. Or that she wasn't worried about them.

Them. They had been a them for over a year now. She liked being a them: meeting at school, Curt would always be waiting for her to get off the bus, having lunch together, he would give her his chips and she would split her sandwich, walking down to the lake and skidding rocks out on the ice, seeing who could get one to glide the farthest and checking in a few times a day when they were apart. But lately things weren't quite the same— Curt had changed.

Where was her good old boyfriend Curt? What had Andy Hindquist done with him?

At first she had been glad when Andy and Curt had started to hang out. Curt seemed happier, more involved in things. Andy had all the latest electronic toys and Curt was so excited about playing with them. Curt's family wouldn't waste their money on them, nor did they allow those violent games in their house. At first Meg had thought that was such a rigid way of looking at videogames, but now she was starting to agree with it.

Since Curt had started playing videogames, it was all he wanted to do. He was obsessed with them. All he wanted to do anymore was go over to Andy's and play them. He didn't mind if Meg came along and for a while she had, but she didn't like playing the games and there was nothing else for her to do. She would sit and watch Curt turn into someone she didn't know and she wasn't sure she liked.

Maybe she should just call him and ask him to go to a movie with her. She loved watching movies with him—they would sit really close to the movie screen, hunker down in the seats, hold hands, eat candy and popcorn, and then afterwards, dissect everything about the movie.

Meg felt hesitant to call him, like she was chasing him, but that was so stupid because she always called him. At least as often as he called her. She never paid attention to things like that before, like who called who last or who called the most, keeping track.

She picked up her cellphone and pressed his code. The phone rang a couple times and then a breathless Curt answered it. "Hey, Meggly."

"Hey, Curtly."

"What's up?"

"I don't know, I was just wondering what you were doing on this blastedly cold day."

"Man, it's like below below out there. I've never seen the red go so low before. I think it was almost thirty below, seriously."

"No way."

"Really way."

Meg smiled. She loved the way they talked to each other. She loved his various names for her. "Are you brave enough to venture out into this weather?"

"What were you thinking?"

"I don't know. I'm just going stark raving trapped in my room. I thought maybe a flick."

"Could be good. I might should check in with Danger Man."

Meg hated that Curt had a special name for Andy and she especially hated what it was. So stupid, Danger Man. Like he was one of the Fantastic Four or something. And Andy called Curt, Mr. Frantic. Unfortunately, Meg was afraid Andy wanted her to be called Invisible Woman. She wasn't going to let that happen.

"Sure," she said, making her voice calm and light. "Yeah, maybe he'd like to go with us."

Curt gave a laugh-growl. "Doubt it, but we had talked about getting together. Why don't I call you later?"

Meg's heart sank. Then she'd just be waiting by the phone again. "Oh, maybe we should forget it."

"No, no. He's not even home yet. Who knows if Andy's even going to be around today He hinted at some hot date. Let's say we're going and if he calls, I'll just tell him, later. I'll be there."

"Okay." Meg felt relieved and yet uneasy. It still felt like Andy came first, that Andy had first dibs on her boyfriend. "Let's try to get in to Red Wing for the early evening show. It's a school night."

Maybe she should become Invisible Woman and fight the Danger Man on his own territory. Maybe she needed to pull out the secret weapon that only women have. The one that she knew Curt had wanted her to use for a long time.

2:30 pm

Amy opened the door to the Walkers' house with the key Sherri had given her.

She took off her wet boots and set them on the mat by the door and then walked into the living room, pulling on neoprene gloves. She didn't have any blue booties, her socks would have to do. First, she'd just do a walk-through, see if anything jumped out at her.

Before she started her search, she stood in the middle of the main floor and looked around. What struck her about the interior of the house was how coordinated the color was—everything was red, white or blue—the couch was blue, the pillows were red, the large rug in the living room was all three colors. How very patriotic, she thought. Maybe that's what you did if you had money and a summer home—you made it look like it was always the Fourth of July. All Amy's furniture had been hand-me-downs so she had given no thought to what color anything was. If it was free, not too beat up, and it didn't stink, she would take it.

Amy went up the curving stairs, which led to the master bedroom, the only room at the top of the house. The space was as big as her whole apartment, with a Jacuzzi-style bathtub set right in front of the windows.

The view was to die for. Amy walked up to the window and felt like she was going to fall the 400 feet down to the snow-covered lake. She wasn't sure she could fall asleep in a room like this, although it would be fun to try.

The bed was dressed with only plain white sheets. She had come up here and pulled the down comforter off the bed to wrap Mr. Walker in. But even the sheets looked expensive, crisp and tightly woven.

Amy couldn't help feeling like she shouldn't be there, even though it was her job. She remembered when she had broken into a house when she was just a kid, not even five years old. She had done it with an older friend. They had gone into the neighbor's bedroom and put on some lipstick. When they had been found, the evidence was right there on her face, bright red and smeared.

The other problem was she didn't really know what she was looking for. If someone had locked Daniel Walker out of his house, that person had more than likely been in the sauna with him. An invited guest. Claire had told her that the Walkers had separated, so conceivably some other woman had been with him. But why would she have locked him out? What would have pushed someone to do such an awful thing?

Of course, if Amy knew the why, she'd know everything. The longer she worked in law enforcement, the more she realized that even the perps didn't always know why they did something.

Funny how on television and in books the criminals seemed so smart. Amy had found they were rarely that.

So she should be looking for any evidence of another person, probably a female, in the house.

Amy opened the drawer of the bedside table and wasn't surprised to find the usual paraphanelia: lotion, nail clippers, Kleenex, aspirin, and lubricant. No diary, unfortunately. No little black book.

A stack of towels were at the head of the bathtub folded neatly on a chair. A rumpled pile of damp towels were next to the tub, obviously just tossed there. Mr. Walker must be used to having other people pick up after him. Might be a good idea to have the towels checked for hair—if a woman was visiting she might well have taken a bath. Amy looked in the tub and noticed a ring of hair and grunge. They could collect those too.

After a quick perusal of the rest of the drawers, which turned up only clothes, she walked down the stairs to the main floor.

In the kitchen she found dishes in the sink, not much in the refrigerator—salami, a jar of mayonnaise, pickles, a six-pack of beer, and some moldy cheese. No signs of lipstick on any of the glasses. But they'd all have to be fingerprinted. An opened box of crackers sat on the counter, a jar of peanut butter with a sticky knife next to it. He certainly was batching it.

She scanned the dining room and living room, but didn't see anything out of the ordinary.

Time to go down to the basement and check out the sauna. The bottom floor wasn't really a basement as only part of it was underground. The side toward the lake was a walkout, with the sauna built in next to the back door.

She opened the door to the sauna and sniffed. The cedar smelled wonderful, deep and tangy like a pine forest after a rain. The room was large enough to fit six people comfortably. A bench ran the length of the room with a small sauna heater, rocks sitting in the top of it.

Three objects sat on the bench: an ashtray with the butt end of a cigar perched on it, a half-empty bottle of expensive vodka and a glass etched with the letter W. So far no trace of anyone but Walker's presence.

As she was backing out of the sauna, Amy heard a clicking noise coming from upstairs—it must be coming from the front door on the main floor. She had purposely locked the door behind her when she came in so it had to be someone who had a key—maybe Daniel Walker's daughter. Amy also knew her presence would not be a secret as her squad car was parked in the driveway.

She ran up the stairs and was surprised to see Sara Hegstrom carrying a vacuum cleaner and a bucket of cleaning equipment. Amy had heard that Sara was supplementing their farm income by doing housekeeping. While she didn't know the woman very well, her dad was friends with Sara's husband Clyde.

"Sara, stop where you are. You can't come in. I'm sorry but you can't clean in here today."

Sara set down the vacuum cleaner in the entryway and held the bucket like it was a baby in her arms. "I saw your squad car out front. What's happened? Are the Walkers okay?"

"We're not quite sure yet, but Mr. Walker was locked outside his house last night and has a bad case of hypothermia. He's been taken to the hospital."

"Oh, no. That's terrible. How could that have happened? Didn't he know better than to go out in this weather?"

"That's a good question. We're not sure what happened, but for now this is being treated as a crime scene."

"Crime? Did someone do this to him? Is he going to be okay?"

"They're not sure."

Sara looked dazed as she leaned against the wall by the front door. "My daughter's at the hospital, too."

"Bonnie?"

"Yes, you know her?"

"Not very well, but I remember her from school even though she was quite a few grades behind me. With her big laugh she was not easy to miss. I'm sorry to hear she's in the hospital. What's going on?"

Sara sat down in the entry hall floor as if all the air had escaped from her. "Oh, she wasn't feeling well. We didn't know. She complained of abdominal cramps. I didn't pay that much attention to her, figured it was just her period. She's always had bad and irregular periods. Then the baby came early."

"She had a baby?"

"I know. Unbelievable." The words rushed out of Sara as if she couldn't even stop them. "Bonnie was at home in bed. Only my husband was there. The baby just came off the ventilator, but Bonnie's not doing so well. I still can't believe it. How could she be pregnant and I didn't even know it? I'm her mother.

What's wrong with me that I didn't know that? But I'm not sure she even knew herself. I've heard of such things happening—but to my daughter?"

Amy wondered who the father was. If her calculations were right, Bonnie was about seventeen years old, last year of high school. "Yes, I've seen it all in this job. What is the baby—a boy or a girl?"

"The sweetest little boy. But he only weighed four pounds when he was born. And Bonnie lost so much blood she went into a coma. She hasn't come out of it yet. But we're hopeful. The doctors say she'll recover."

"How's the baby?"

Sara's face lit up. "Even though he came early, he's perfect. He has little tufts of red hair too." She wiped her face and stood up. "I suppose I should get going back to the hospital." She gathered up her gear and looked around at the house. "When will I be able to clean?

"I'm not sure. But probably within a day or two. How long have you been cleaning for the Walkers?"

"The last couple years. They're pretty easy to clean for, or they were before they separated. Mr. Walker, on his own, is a slob."

"Do you know why they separated?"

"Not really, but I could guess. Mr. Walker has a roving eye, if you know what I mean."

"Did he ever try anything with you?"

"No, thank god. I think I'm too old for him."

CHAPTER 6
New Year's Day: 3:15 pm

Claire glanced up from the *People* magazine she was still reading—too many pictures of gorgeous women in jeans and big sunglasses—as a tall, model-thin young woman walked into the waiting room.

"Here's Danielle," Sherri whispered.

Danielle certainly knew how to make an entrance—her high-heeled boots clicked on the granite floor, her fur jacket hung open to reveal a low-cut red sweater. The two older women sitting in the corner of the room stared at her as did the young boy slouched in a chair, half asleep. He sat up straight.

The similiarity between this woman and Sherri was striking. Both women were tall and thin with long honey-colored hair. They both wore high-heeled footwear. Lipstick was a must for both of them—Sherri went for a dark deep red, Danielle wore a glistening pink.

Claire watched Danielle scan the room, catch sight of Sherri, and then narrow her eyes and stalk over.

"What did you do to my dad?" were the first words out of Danielle's mouth. Claire noticed how she claimed Dan Walker.

"Let's step outside," Sherri suggested. "That way I can tell you what's going on and not bother everyone else."

"No. I don't care who hears this. I want to see my father and I want to know what happened to him. Figures you'd be the one to find him since you were probably responsible for what happened." Danielle leaned in close to Sherri and spat her words in her face. "What did you do to him?"

Much as she wanted to hear more of what Danielle had to say, Claire stood and put a restraining hand on the young woman's shoulder. "Calm down. You can't see your father right now, but he's in good hands."

"Well, you're who I should be talking to anyway. This woman," Danielle pointed at Sherri, "stood to gain a lot by my father's death. You're a cop. I'm guessing she had something to do with my dad getting hurt or almost killed."

"I don't need to listen to this." Sherri stood up and left the room.

The two older women leaned forward, continuing to listen intently to the conversation.

"No need to be accusing anyone of anything. We don't know what happened yet." Claire then insisted, "Sit down and I'll tell you what's going on."

Danielle plunked down next to Claire and set her plump pink leather purse in her lap as if it was a fat cat that needed to be petted. Danielle's lips curled back and she said quietly, "I can make a pretty good guess."

"Don't you want to know how your father is?"

For a moment, Danielle turned into a little girl, her lips quivered and her eyes filled with tears. "Is he okay? Did he really almost freeze to death? How could that happen? Is he going to be okay?"

"So far so good. The doctors have to take it very slowly in warming him up. So we won't know for a while."

Danielle looked at Claire. "You mean, he still could die?"

"There's a chance, but I think he's in pretty good hands."

The young woman hung her head, her hair cascading down over her face. "I can't believe this could happen to him. I'm sure he didn't lock himself out of the house, he doesn't do things like that."

"Why would you think Sherri would do anything to your father?" Claire asked in a low voice.

Danielle lifted her head, flicked back her hair, and sniffed back her tears. "Stupid cow. They're getting a divorce. He was dumping her without a cent. If he were to die before the divorce, she probably thinks she would get everything."

4:10 pm

Curt sank into the bean bag next to Andy's and grabbed the controls. They were going for the record. What a way to start the new year!

Curt loved the way Andy had his room set up so he didn't even have to get out of bed to play. He had everything he needed within reach: all his games and the controllers sat on a long bench at the foot of the bed. He had blinds that stayed permanently down on his windows so that it was nice and dark and you could see the screen better. The low light of the game revealed walls covered with posters of old bands—Nirvana, Def Leppard, the Doors. He even had a lava lamp that burbled away in the corner.

Andy didn't turn his head to talk to Curt. He just gave a nod and said, "I got it, man. I told you I would."

"What?"

"You know, that other version of GTA."

Curt always had to remind himself that GTA wasn't a grocery store chain, it was the best video game in the world, Grand Theft Auto. "Remind me."

"I told you about it—that Hot Coffee version, where they left in the sex scenes. I managed to score a copy in the cities this morning. You ready to crack it?"

"I guess." Curt didn't want to admit he felt a little weird watching sex scenes with other guys. He would probably feel weird watching sex scenes period, but maybe if he was by himself he could get into them more.

After playing the game for a while, he found that the sex scenes didn't bother him that much. They were just a part of the whole intensity of the action. He felt himself sinking into the game, after a few false moves, getting himself killed in stupid ways, he started to figure it out and a smoothness entered him. He felt like he could play the game forever.

When he finally got killed again, he pulled his gaze away from the monitor and glanced over at the clock radio by Andy's bed. "It's really after four o'clock?"

"Time flies when you're crushing the bad guys." Andy laughed.

"I gotta go, man."

"Hear ya," Andy didn't even look at him, still focusing on the game.

"Cool game," Curt said.

"Yeah, back at ya."

Curt laughed. When it was just the two of them, they threw the hip-hop slang at each other. Just for fun. Just to try it out. "Round."

"Yeah, later."

Curt reluctantly stood up. As he unfolded his body from the bean bag, he couldn't believe he had been sitting in the same position for over three hours. Amazing how time went by when you were trying to steal a bunch of cars!

Then it hit him—he remembered Meg and the movie they were going to see. He was supposed to be at her house right now; she had wanted to grab something to eat before the movie. He thought of completely blowing her off, rather than going over there now and facing her. It would not be pretty. She was not going to let him forget this.

4:30 pm

Amy walked slowly through the house one last time and didn't see anything else jump out at her.

As far as she could tell, Dan Walker hadn't had a guest last night, but had, in fact, celebrated the new year alone. Unless that person didn't eat, drink, smoke, or leave anything behind. Maybe they had cleaned up after themselves, although seeing the mess in the sink, she didn't see how that would be possible.

She walked up to the bank of windows on the main floor and stared outside at the top of the trees. Even in the warmth of the house, she could tell how cold it was outside. The trees moved differently, more rigidly, like they would snap if you touched them. And the snow had a brittle quality. When it was blown up by the wind, it swirled in a tight tornado of sharp shards. Dangerous weather.

Amy didn't want to go back outside. She wanted to lay down on the Berber carpet and sleep. What she really wanted to do was turn on the sauna, take all her clothes off, and sit in that small cedar room until her bones melted.

When she turned away from the windows, she saw a stack of papers tucked on a shelf under the coffee table. They looked legal. She pulled them out and glanced over them.

"Purchase agreement," it read across the top of the page. She scanned the first sheet and saw the name of Edna Gordon, then the block and lot numbers of her farm. What was this about?

Amy realized what she was holding in her hands was an agreement for Daniel Walker to buy the Gordon farm. For a chunk of change, but, by what she knew about the real estate market, not quite what it was worth, even though the market wasn't as good as it had been.

She couldn't believe that Walker had been able to talk Edna into selling the family farm.

Amy had a hard time believing that John Gordon would have let that land go under any circumstances. From the little she knew of their situation, John was actually working other jobs just to keep the farm together. She heard he had gone south to work in construction this winter. Maybe it had all gotten to be too much for him. Maybe the agreement was totally legit.

Or maybe Daniel Walker had sweet-talked Edna into selling the farm when John hadn't been around, maybe he had given someone else a good reason to want him dead.

CHAPTER 7

4:30 pm

Rich finished making a bed of straw for Meg's goat. A stray cat wound around his legs. The scrawny creature had made a home for himself in the barn and Rich had bought a bag of cat food to feed him. This morning when he had come out to the barn, he had found the goat and the cat curled up together.

As he stood, he felt his back twinge. Time to take a break. Rich decided to treat himself at Le Pain Perdu to a French donut or two and a cup of coffee. He needed the warmth, he needed the sustenance, but what he really needed was some company. He had heard that the bakery was going to be open on New Year's Day. Besides serving baked goods Stuart had promised to be offering black-eyed peas and rice, a traditional fare for the day from the other end of the Mississippi.

When he stepped outside, he felt his shoulders go into a hunch and the wind swept his breath away. Working in the barn Rich had been at least sheltered from the wind, but it was still nasty cold. His fingers were red and swollen and his ankles itched. He remembered his mom talking about chilblains that she had gotten in the winter when she was a kid, a skin affliction that came from your skin freezing and thawing. He'd have to talk to Claire's sister Bridget, the pharmacist, about what he could put on his skin.

When Rich drove up to the bakery, he pulled his pickup truck as close as he could get to the sidewalk without getting stuck in the snowbank. The snow had been piled up next to the curb by the plow and Stuart had, at least, cut a path through it to get to the bakery.

As Rich pushed open the frosted door to Le Pain Perdu, warmth and humidity hit him in the face. Then the delectable smells. In the cold outdoor air of January all odors went away, but inside the bakery the air was filled with cardamon, cinnamon, and almond fragrances. He wanted it all.

But first he needed a big cup of coffee. He walked over to a stack of cups and picked the largest one he could find, then pulled the coffee pot off the burner and poured himself a brimming cup.

"Who said you could help yourself?" the waitress, Cheryl he thought her name was, swatted him with a towel.

"Hey, if I had to wait for the service around here, I'd never get anything."

"Just for that, we're out of French donuts."

"Don't tell me that. I might have to go back out into the cold, sit in a snowbank, and pout."

"We might have one or two left."

"Make it three, please. I'll seat myself." Rich went over to his favorite spot, the booth by the south-facing window. He knew he was getting no vitamin D from the sun at this time of year, but the brightness and the faint sense of heat would have to do.

"Rich, my man." Stuart Lewis, the blond, svelte owner of the bakery, slid into the booth opposite him. How Stuart managed to keep so thin when he was always around all these sweets was amazing to Rich. But he knew that Stuart worked at it. Rich would sometimes see him running to the bakery at four in the morning. Stuart had explained that he had to exercise hard and consistently or all the pastries he ate would make him the Michelin man.

"Cold enough for you?" Rich asked the typical January question. "You didn't run to work today, did you?"

"No way. Actually I wish it would drop another ten degrees. Isn't that the point were the gas freezes in the tank? Then, at least, I'd have an excuse for staying home. It was bitter this morning."

Cheryl set a plate of three French donuts in front of Rich and poured him another blast of coffee. Rich nodded thanks. She lifted the pot in Stuart's direction and he nodded yes. She went to get him a cup.

"What's going on?" Rich asked, again a reflex question. He figured that way Stuart could talk while he stuffed the first donut in his mouth.

"Well, I just heard that Dan Walker landed in the hospital. They say he tried to turn into the abominable snowman. Claire's there with him so I'm guessing it must have been more than an accident. You heard anything?"

Cheryl set down Stuart's coffee in his special mug marked, "King Rolling Pin."

Rich shook his head. "You know I'm always the last to know these things. Claire might mention something about work when she gets home. If she thinks about it or if I ask."

"I only know because the EMTs who took him to the hospital stopped by for coffee."

"What happened? Hypothermia? What'd the idiot do—go for a walk last night and get lost?"

"Yeah, without any clothes on."

"You're kidding. Although I've heard people who get hypothermia often pull all their clothes off."

"No, I guess he was trying out his new sauna and decided to go for a roll in the snow."

"He sure picked the wrong night. But I don't get why Claire's involved."

"I heard they suspect that his wife might have locked him out."

"Yikes, that's rather serious. I have to admit I didn't care for the guy myself, but there might be better ways to settle their differences."

"Sara Hegstrom told me she thinks they're getting divorced. She cleans house for them. She says they've been at each other."

"Boy, you are gossip central today."

"Gotta do something to keep your mind off the weather." Stuart looked down at the last donut on Rich's plate. "How're the donuts today?"

"Slightly above average, which is pretty darn good in my book."

Stuart was starting to walk away when Rich stopped him. "Hey, I have news."

"What's that?"

Rich had to tell someone. "Claire popped the question last night."

"What question? What's the meaning of life?"

"No, the other question. She asked me to marry her."

Stuart snorted. "Marriage? Aren't you guys past that?"

"Not me. Her pension might come in handy down the road." Rich smiled. "You up to baking a cake?"

4:45 pm

Amy had forgotten how attractive John Gordon was. Not in a dark, tall, conventional way. He was short and stocky with sandy red hair, light blue eyes, ruddy skin—but he was so healthy looking, so strong, so full of life. She also had forgotten how brusque he could be.

When she had knocked on his mother's front door, he had pulled it open with a, "What do you want?"

"Can I come in?"

He had simply stepped back and gotten out of her way.

Amy entered through the back door, which was the door everyone used to enter the farmhouse and led right into the kitchen. A large round oak table was in the middle of the floor with chairs around it and a lazy susan in the middle, holding salt and pepper and condiments. There was a glow to the room: the sun streaming in the window over the sink, the old cookstove putting out heat, and the companionship of the two people in it.

Edna turned from the stove and said, "Well, if it isn't little Amy. Haven't seen you in an age."

"Hey, Mrs. Gordon," Amy said, watching the older woman get a coffee cup down from the shelf. She hadn't seen Edna Gordon in several years, and she knew Edna must be getting close to eighty, although she looked quite good and seemed to move around easily. Her short, blunt-cut hair still had a smattering of brown in it and her blue eyes seemed as clear as day.

Without even asking Amy if she wanted a cup of coffee, Edna poured her one and set it down on the table. "Have a chair. Talk to John while I go get another chair. I'll be right back."

"I don't know if you have heard what's happened to your neighbor, Daniel Walker?" As Amy said this she watched John pretty carefully to see how he would react to her question.

He blew up. "Don't even say that asshole's name in this house. He is the biggest slime bag I know. Makes like he's your friend and then stabs you in the back. What happened? Did his Mercedes get stuck in a snowbank?"

"No, he got locked out of his house last night and almost froze to death. He's in the hospital in intensive care."

John deflated. He sank down into his chair opposite her and stared at her. "How'd he manage that?"

"Well, it appears he was taking a sauna, went outside to cool off, and didn't get back into the house."

"Wow. Did he lock himself out?"

Amy wasn't sure how much she should tell them. Better to say less. "We're not sure."

"Is he going to make it?" John's voice sounded like he wasn't sure what answer he wanted.

"It's looking like he's going to be all right. Still a little early to tell. Like I said, he's in the hospital and they're in the process of warming him up." Amy shook her head at the memory. "I thought he was dead when I saw him."

Edna came back in with her chair, then poured her more coffee and put a hand on her shoulder. "Something happen to Dan?"

"He almost frozen to death," John told her.

"He's not a very nice man," Edna remarked.

"I don't really know him," Amy said. "What is he like? Obviously, you don't care for him too much."

"You got that right. I'd like to wring his thick neck, but that doesn't mean I'd actually do anything about it. I did some work for him but I sure wouldn't work for him again. Dan, well, let's just say, he takes advantage of people." John seemed oblivious to the fact that he might be a suspect.

Amy took a sip of coffee and then said, "When I was over at the house, looking around I found the purchase agreement. I hadn't realized that you were thinking about selling the farm."

John's shoulders sank.

Edna stood up straight by the stove. "That was all my fault, Amy. I thought I was doing the right thing. I've been such a burden to John lately. Can't keep up my end of things anymore. In this weather I'm stuck out here, can't even drive. I thought if we sold the place, John could get on with his life, not worry about farming anymore, not worry about me or this place. I could move to Pepin, one of those little apartments. It'd be easier for him."

"Mom, for once and for all, you're not a burden. Plus, you'd go crazy in Pepin. You know it." John sighed. "Yeah, while I was gone this fall, Dan made an offer for the farm and my mom signed it away."

"You sure there's nothing you can do to get it back?" Amy asked.

"I've got a lawyer checking into it."

Edna said, "Maybe you could have me declared mentally incompetent and that would null and void the contract."

John gave a sharp bark of a laugh. "Mom, you've not only got all your marbles, you're still winning the game with them. Don't think anyone would buy that."

Edna looked happy. "How nice of you to say."

Amy wished she could sit for the rest of the afternoon in this cozy kitchen, drinking coffee and shooting the bull with Edna and John, but duty called. "Well, I just wondered if you noticed anything strange last night. Anyone driving down the Walkers' driveway."

"I was in bed by nine per usual. What about you, John? You stayed up to watch the news, didn't you?"

"Yeah, but then I tucked in right after that. I don't recall seeing anyone over to their place. We can only see the start of the driveway, by the time it drops down close to the house, we don't see it anymore."

"Well, if you think of anything, let me know."

John rubbed his forehead. "So you're actually thinking someone did this to him? That someone was responsible for what happened to Dan?"

"We're not sure. Just checking all possibilities."

"Can't he tell you himself?"

"He's not come around yet. Maybe later today we'll know what went on." Amy finished her coffee and stood up. "Thanks for the joe."

"You keep us posted on what's going on with Mr. Walker," Edna said. "Maybe he'll forget he even wants the farm."

5:30 pm

Claire stood in the hospital room doorway, watching Sherri Walker approach the bed where her husband lay stretched out, wires pasted to his chest and a tube going into his lower abdomen. As his wife leaned over him, Dan Walker stirred, mouthing something, then faded back into slumber, or something deeper, coma.

Sherri stood still, a hand on his forehead, then turned back and looked at Claire. "Did you see that?"

Claire nodded.

Sherri's eyes widened and her voice sounded hopeful. "I think he's coming out of it."

"Looks like it." Claire couldn't help but wonder when he would be in good enough shape to talk. But she knew she was jumping ahead of herself.

She had originally assumed that if anyone had locked Mr. Walker out of his house, it most probably would have been his wife, soon to be ex-wife. Having Danielle come flouncing in and give Sherri the best motive in the world for trying to get him out of the way before the divorce went through certainly enhanced that speculation.

But after Danielle had left for the cafeteria to get herself a cup of coffee, Sherri had talked a bit about what had happened between her and Dan. Not trying to persuade Claire of anything; more, it seemed, to try to figure it out in her own mind.

"Dan just seems to always need something new to focus on. Like the cabin, once it was done, it didn't interest him much anymore. Putting in the sauna this fall helped. His latest project. I think for a while I was his project, but then I was old hat. He needed someone new. It's just the way he is. I'm not even sure he can help it."

Claire thought of Rich, who always seemed so content doing what he had always done—raise pheasants—but doing it well, improving on it if he could. In the same way, he had never given up on her, staying steady and strong as she sometimes struggled with her life. "Sounds like a hard way to live."

Sherri had nodded. "It is. I hated it. But, surprisingly, I think it is hard on Dan, too."

"How so?" Claire had said.

"Well, he's not getting any younger and he can't go at everything as strongly as he used to be able to. I think he feels that sometimes and he gets down about it, feels he has to prove himself."

Now watching Sherri attentively leaning over her husband, trying to urge him back into the world of the living, Claire questioned her original take on the woman. Plus, as Amy had pointed out, why would she have told them about the dead bolt being locked if she was the one who had done it. Otherwise, they might have assumed it was an accident.

"I think he saw me," Sherri said, "He was trying to say something. Did you see that?"

The woman had such a hopeful look in her eyes that Claire hated to do anything but agree. "Yes, that's what it looked like."

"I'm just going to stay here with him. If that's okay," Sherri said, reaching out to touch her husband's cheek.

"I can't leave you alone with him," Claire forced herself to say.

Sherri turned, her eyes widened, her mouth stretching tight as she seemed to realize the implications of Claire's words.

CHAPTER 8

New Year's Day: 6 pm

Clyde sat in a lounge chair next to his daughter's bed, sipped the lukewarm coffee and pretended it was full of flavor. Bonnie was sleeping. She was still recovering from her blood loss and seemed very weak. She drifted in and out of being. Sometimes she would jolt awake and ask for the baby. At the moment, her eyes were closed but he wondered if she was really sleeping or just avoiding being awake.

He couldn't help remembering what had happened two mornings ago. After his wife left for work, he had hollered down the stairs to wake Bonnie. He was surprised that she wasn't dressed and sitting at the table, eating some sugary cereal. She was usually up bright and early for school.

When Clyde still didn't hear her moving about in her room, he went down to make sure she was awake. He knocked on her door, and that's when he heard the groans. "Bonnie?"

She yelled through the door, "Dad, help me."

When he pushed the door open, he couldn't make out what he was seeing. Bonnie looked like she was struggling with something in the bed. She was groaning and crying and pulled at something that was between her legs.

At first he had thought there was a small animal in bed with her, a squirrel that had maybe come in the dryer vent. As he walked closer, he saw the small creature was still attached to his daughter by the umbilical cord. A huge pool of blood had soaked into the mattress.

"Dad," she sobbed, her face red with exhaustion and smeared blood. "I'm having a baby."

His heart stopped and he couldn't figure out how this could be. They hadn't even known Bonnie was pregnant. She was only seventeen. She didn't even have a boyfriend. Yes, she had been putting on the pounds lately, but not bad. She had always been a little chunky. How could this be?

"I'd say you've already had it." He had to do something. Unfortunately, his wife had already left for work.

"But I won't stop bleeding," Bonnie said faintly.

From birthing many calves he knew what to do. He lifted the small form and that was when he realized it wasn't breathing. As long as the baby was still attached to its mother it would be okay, but they needed help.

He handed the baby to his daughter and then asked, "Who did this to you?"

"Don't tell Mom."

He nodded.

She whispered a name and then he went to call an ambulance.

7:00 pm

Meg slumped down into the seat in the movie theater. A handful of kids and their parents were sprinkled around the seats behind her. She liked to sit close to the front. That way she felt like she was part of the movie, she could fall into it, not know where the film began and she ended.

Curt understood this feeling. But, at the moment for whatever reason, he wasn't sitting next to her.

She had waited for him for a half an hour at her house and then she left for Red Wing, but not in time to catch the first show. She wasn't going to call him, track him down. She was pretty sure she knew where he was—with Andy. Curt was a big boy and he could take care of himself. Or not.

But Meg was really mad. How could he do this to her? After all they'd been through. He was like her soul mate, her perfect match, and now he was changing into someone she didn't even know.

She grabbed a handful of popcorn and started eating it, but even that reminded her of Curt. He called her style of eating popcorn, *pecking*. With her lips she would pluck one popped kernel out of her hand and eat it—like a chicken eating feed. She told him it was just her way of enjoying every single bite.

The trailers started. She loved trailers, those teasers of coming movies. She even liked the ads that showed in front of the movies. The movie she had picked was a new one, just out: *Coraline*. She didn't know what it was about but she knew it was animated, which Curt loved, obviously, and rather creepy, which they both loved.

Meg sunk deeper into the seat as the movie started. This odd scrawny girl had just moved into an odd scrawny house with a geeky boy living there and his odd scrawny smart cat. So far so good. And the girl's parents didn't understand or pay attention to her. Sometimes Meg felt that way, but not too often. Then the girl, Coraline, started yelling at the geeky boy and Meg really relished that part. Stupid boys!

Suddenly two hands covered her eyes. She let out a small peep.

Curt's voice whispered in her ear. "I found you." He climbed over the seat back and slid in next to her.

She gave him a glare. "I wasn't lost."

"You mad?"

"I'm watching the movie."

"It looks good."

"Sh-sh."

"Can I have some popcorn?"

She was tempted to tell him to get his own, but decided that would be silly and result in more disruption and so she shoved the box at him, causing a few precious kernels to fall on the floor.

"Thanks," he said.

It was hard to focus on the movie with Curt sitting next to her. She kept having imaginary conversations with him in her mind: ones in which she told him off, ones in which he begged her forgiveness and promised never to see Andy again, even one in which he told her he had been in a bad car accident and almost lost his life, but had managed to crawl out of the wreckage and come and find her. Most of them ended with the two of them kissing.

At least Curt didn't try to hold her hand. They always held hands during movies, but he seemed to know not to even try that. When he went to give her the popcorn back, she just pushed it away. She wasn't really hungry anymore.

In the meantime, Coraline was having a rough time. She had found a secret door in the wall, which led to a parellel world that at first appeared to be perfect, but then the cracks started to show. With the help of the scrawny cat and the geeky guy, she managed to thwart the evil witch-type lady, Belle Dame, and get her real life back, spacey parents and all.

Meg wondered if something similar was happening between her and Curt—she had thought he was perfect and now she was seeing his warts. Maybe what she needed to do was kiss him more often so he wouldn't be such a frog, but she sure didn't feel like doing it now.

When the movie ended they didn't stand up immediately. They sat there as the lights came up.

Curt said, "Cool animation."

"I didn't like the tunnel between the two worlds. It looked like an old dryer vent tube," Meg blurted out, even though she usually had a rule—no comments on the movie until they were safely in the car.

She stood up and started walking out of the theater. Curt followed her. When they got out to the hallway, he tried to swing his arm onto her shoulder, but she shrugged out from under it.

"Hey, listen," he said. "We need to talk. Why don't we go get a cup of coffee at the Jenny?"

"I need to get home."

"Meg, don't do this to me."

She felt her anger burbling inside of her. She turned on him and yelled in a quiet voice, "Excuse me. Who did what to whom?"

"Whoa. What's the matter with you?"

"I don't like being stood up."

"The time slipped away…"

"I can guess where you were," Meg said, hoping he'd tell her differently.

But he didn't say anything. Just looked down and shuffled his shoes.

"I gotta get home," she said and turned toward the parking lot. "It's a school night."

"Too bad we can't drive together," he said.

"You should have thought of that a few hours ago," she said and walked away.

He didn't try to stop her; he didn't come running after her. She climbed into her car and was happy when it started on the first try. She sat and let it run, but didn't even bother to turn the heat on yet. It would just blow frigid air at her.

She watched Curt walk to his truck, his shoulders hunched inside his thin jacket. He never wore enough clothes. She had knit him a scarf for Christmas and she could see that he had that wrapped around his neck.

What was the matter with boys? Don't they even know enough to say they're sorry when they mess up? That's all she had wanted to hear from him, but he hadn't known enough to apologize.

7:30 pm

"Where's Meg?" Claire asked as she walked in the living room and saw only Rich sitting by the fire.

"Well, hey to you too." Rich laughed. "I think she went into Red Wing to see a movie with Curt."

Claire walked over and tilted his head back and gave him a just-came-out-of-the-cold kiss on the lips. "Those two. They're so serious. Makes me nervous." Then she tried to slide her hands down the neck of his flannel shirt to warm them up.

"Don't you dare put your cold hands on me." Rich grabbed her around the neck and pulled her down for another, deeper kiss, then said, "Curt's a nice kid. Relax. It's always intense at that age."

"I guess. How about our age? I'm freezing here. You need to warm me up." Claire wrapped her arms around him.

"Well, I've been thinking about that. As I recall you propositioned me the other night."

"Correction. Let's get it straight. After much consideration, I proposed to you. Just wanted to make you an honest man."

"Yes, and after equally careful consideration, taking into account all your hard work and effort in bringing some couth to my simple life, I've decided to take you up on it. My answer is yes." Rich pulled her down into his lap.

Claire felt something inside of her grow warm and sank into his kiss. Finally, she pulled away from him and said, "Good. Should we set a date?"

Rich snuggled his head into her neck and whispered in her ear. "Sure. When would you like?"

"Something easy to remember. How about Valentine's Day?"

"I think that can be arranged."

"Let's keep it simple. Not too many people."

Rich laughed. "What're you talking about? We'll do it just

like all the other weddings around here. We'll put a notice in the paper inviting everyone in the county and see who shows up."

"I like it."

"Hey, how's your abominable snowman?"

"Daniel Walker?"

"You have more than one?"

"He appears to be out of danger," Claire rested her head against Rich's chest and put her feet up next to his on the ottoman. She could feel the fire's heat on the bottom of her feet. "But when I left the hospital, he still hadn't come around yet. Did you hear that he and his wife were separated?"

"Suspicious."

Claire looked over at Rich, his face lit by the fire. He was wearing the red skullcap that Meg had knit him for Christmas pulled down to his ears. Claire thought he looked like a lumberjack, but a cute, good-hearted one. "Yeah, maybe."

"So is it true that someone locked him out of his house? And was he really naked?" Rich asked.

"How'd you hear all that?"

"Donuts," he explained.

Claire shook her head, then let it fall back on the chair. "After all these years, I still can't get over how news travels around here."

"What else have we got to do but talk about each other?"

"Point taken. As far as Walker goes, all we've got is his wife's word for it that the dead bolt on the back door was locked. But I can think of no reason why she would lie about that."

"How can someone do that? Freeze and then come back to life."

"How they do it is very slowly, by what I saw today in the hospital. And very carefully. They cut a hole in his stomach, then gently washed his innards with warm water."

"Really? A hole in his stomach? Amazing. Is he going to lose anything to frostbite?"

"Hard to tell. The doctor said he might lose part of an ear and a couple toes. I can't believe he is coming through this as well as he is."

"The body is a remarkable machine." Rich thought for a second, then added, "Course I've seen piglets come back to life after they were frozen. I guess it might have helped that Daniel Walker was a bit of a pig."

"Rich, you don't like the guy?" Claire asked, not a bit surprised that he didn't like Walker, but surprised that he would express it so clearly. Even with her, he didn't usually say much negative about anyone.

"He doesn't care for anyone but himself. Anyway, anyhow. I bet there's ten people right in Fort St. Antoine that wouldn't mind getting rid of him if they thought they could get away with it."

"Could you give me that list?"

He slid his hands under her shirt and said, "Maybe we can strike a deal. I might need some warming up myself."

CHAPTER 9

2 January: 9 am

I tell you what, that man must not have the sense that god gave geese. Who'd a guessed that a sauna needed to come with operating instructions," Sheriff Talbert said as he sat stuffed into his swivel chair.

Claire was worried about the sheriff. He had gained weight over the holidays—just like everyone else in the department—in the county for that matter—but those extra pounds on top of the others that he had been accumulating for the last few years were not looking good. His face was constantly flushed and he wheezed. He was approaching sixty-five years old and his age wasn't sitting well with him. But she couldn't imagine the sheriff's department without him.

"We just about lost Mr. Daniel Walker," Claire said. "If that new woman doctor up at the hospital hadn't known how to handle hypothermia, he would have been a goner for sure."

Sheriff Talbert winced. "How'd his privates come through the ordeal?"

So like a man to worry about such things. Claire had to cough to keep from laughing. "Well, the doctor didn't mention them. I'm sure they had burrowed deep into his body and were protected."

"Hope so. Makes me shiver just to think about it."

"What I'm concerned about is, well, it's looking like someone tried to kill him. I'm wondering how we should handle this."

"I guess handle it like an attempted homicide."

"Yes, but his wife is, at the moment, number one suspect and she's also the one making decisions about his medical care."

"Well, that's gotta stop. Is there anyone else who could step in?"

"His daughter's there."

"How old is she?"

"I'd guess early twenties." Claire thought about Danielle's attitude. "But somehow I don't trust her even as much as his wife. They seem cut from the same cloth. Skinny women who need to be kept in high style."

"Well, talk to the doctor and keep a close eye on what's going on with him. So you think the wife might have locked him out? That's cold."

"I don't know. She's the logical suspect. She has the most to gain. According to Daniel's daughter, who by the way is named Danielle, if they divorced Sherri wouldn't get a penny, but if Daniel died before the divorce went through she might inherit most everything."

The sheriff pouched his lips, then nodded. "That's certainly a darn good motive. Money'll do it."

"Yes, but something just doesn't feel right to me." Claire had been thinking about this as she drove to work, going over and over what had happened to Daniel Walker in her mind. "First of all, Sherri has no alibi for New Year's Eve. You'd think she'd have planned something if she was going to try to off her husband. Secondly, she was the one who told us the house was locked up with a dead bolt, which could only have been done from the inside or with a key. If she hadn't let us know that, we would have assumed Walker had just had an accident—letting her off the hook. Third, why would she have been the one to find him?"

The sheriff shrugged. "So who did it?"

"Well, as I told you, when Sherri got there the house was locked up tight. I think it all comes down to who had a key."

"To get in and then lock the deadbolt."

"Right. So my mission today is to track down all the keys."

The sheriff tilted back in his chair and Claire worried that he might tip over, but he caught himself. "Better than a needle in a haystack."

9 am

As always, Curt was waiting for Meg when she got off the bus at school. He smiled up at her as if nothing was wrong. His light brown hair was still damp from his shower and he looked happy to see her.

"Hey," he said, bumping her gently with his shoulder. "Good movie last night. I've been wanting to see that one for a while."

"Yeah. It was okay." She didn't stop to bump him back or to tilt her head up for a kiss. She just kept walking.

Curt walked along with her, staying close. "Sorry about last night. I just lost track of time. Andy had this new game, you know. It was pretty cool. I just spaced out, you know."

"I don't know."

"Come on. Lighten up."

She had been all ready to forgive him, after all he had finally said he was sorry, but the 'lighten up' comment got her all mad again. "I don't want to lighten up. I'm kinda serious, if you haven't forgotten that about me. Also I'm serious about you. I think you need to think about how you feel about me. What's more important in your life?" As soon as the words were out of her mouth, Meg wished she could pull them back. She sounded so needy.

"Whoa." Curt stepped back from her as if he was trying to see her from a new angle.

She stalked off and this time Curt didn't follow.

Meg felt like putting her head in her locker and then just climbing in and shutting the door. What a way to start the day. Maybe what was happening between them wasn't all Curt's fault. Maybe she was too serious about everything. What was the matter with her?

Just then Andy walked by and rammed his fist into her shoulder, in what she took to be a friendly tap. The guy didn't realize his own strength, plus he sure didn't know how to treat girls.

"Where's my main man?" he asked.

Meg hated the faux hip-hop lingo. She wanted to say, "Your man is a seventeen-year-old boy who is going to a Podunk school in the smallest county in rural Wisconsin with more cows per capita than any other state. Not a single black person even lives in this county, nor anyone remotely hip. Drop the stupid jive." But instead she pointed to where she had left Curt.

Candy Bjurkquist slid up to her and said, "Did you hear about Bonnie?"

In their small school there was only one Bonnie, Bonnie Hegstrom, who was a year ahead of them in school. Meg barely knew the girl. She was very quiet and rather ponderous. Not unattractive, but not much of a personality. Lately, she seemed to be neglecting herself. Meg noticed that Bonnie had gained weight and her face had broken out and her hair seemed greasy all the time. She hoped Bonnie hadn't had a nervous breakdown or some horrible rare disease that would kill her. She didn't need more bad news today.

As much as she would have liked to have said into Candy's intent face, *I don't gossip,* she couldn't resist asking, "What?"

"She's in the hospital," Candy said with a half smile that said clearly there was more.

"Why?"

"I heard she had a baby."

"No way. She wasn't pregnant, was she?"

"I guess so. Didn't you notice how big her t-shirts were getting?"

"I just thought she was putting on weight."

Candy shook her head. "What I can't figure out is what guy knocked her up? You have any ideas?"

Meg felt sorry for Bonnie. Only seventeen years old and saddled with a baby. Knowing her parents, they'd probably make her keep it. She'd be stuck with a kid and living with her parents the rest of her life. Meg went through a list of possible boys in her head. No one came to mind. Then she wondered about Andy. He lived close to Bonnie, just a couple farms away. He

certainly seemed horny all the time and wasn't going with anyone from school that she knew of, although Curt had said something about a hot date. She'd have to check it out.

Meg shrugged. "Not really. How'd you hear this?"

"My aunt works at the hospital. She says that Bonnie's not
doing so well, kinda scary."

"Wouldn't you be if you were in that situation?"

Candy shrugged. "I guess the baby's cute."

For a second, Meg wished she were closer to Bonnie and
could go the hospital and talk to her, make her feel so not alone.
But she knew she wouldn't feel comfortable doing that. But
maybe there was something else she could do.

She'd have to find a way to check out what Andy knew about
Bonnie, if there was any chance he was the father. Ask Curt
what he knew about Andy's love life. Maybe that would get him
out of Curt's life. Kill two birds with one stone. Andy would
have to stop playing games and start thinking about earning a
living for his new family.

Maybe this was good news after all.

10 am

Amy saw Claire coming down the hall and stood up from where
she had been dozing in a chair, across the hall from Mr. Walker's
room. The hospital felt so warm after the sub-zero weather outside and so quiet with the nurses walking around in their rub-
ber-soled shoes, that she had felt sleep creeping up on her.

She tried to look alert and told Claire, "I haven't seen either
the daughter or the wife yet this morning. They stayed pretty

late last night from what Bill told me. Then, I guess, they got a hotel room."

"Together? They don't seem to care for each other."

"Not sure what the sleeping arrangement was."

Claire's cheeks were rosy and she had a scarf wrapped around her neck over her uniform. "How long have you been here?"

"Not that long. I relieved Billy Boy an hour or so ago."

"How's Walker doing today?"

"I've heard him moaning, but I thought I'd wait for you to come and talk to him. Dr. Cornwall came by about an half hour ago and checked all his vitals. She told me he'd stabilized, in fact, I guess he's doing pretty good, but they've got him rather doped up. She said we could talk to him if we kept it short. She still thought he would lose a couple toes for sure and maybe even a finger or two. But not bad for a guy who was nearly frozen to death."

Claire tucked her hands under her arms as if she was trying to warm them up. "Every year I forget how cold it can get here. I heard down in some of the coulees it was almost 40 below last night."

"My car barely started this morning. Even plugged in."

"Well, let's go see if we can rouse Mr. Walker."

Amy followed Claire into the room. Daniel Walker's face looked like he had been badly burned. Odd how intense cold was similar to fire. Blisters circled his mouth and eyes, his skin was red and cracked open.

Daniel Walker opened his eyes slowly and painfully. Then he took a moment to focus. He stared at Claire's face, moved his head slowly to take in Amy, then looked down at their uniforms. He closed his eyes, then pulled them open again.

He cracked his mouth and whispered some words. Amy couldn't make out what he was saying.

Claire leaned in closer and said, "Could you repeat that?"

He cleared his throat, then asked in a louder, hoarse voice, "What did I do?"

"Don't you remember?" Claire asked.

"I hurt all over. What happened?" His bandaged hand wandered up to his face and he stared at it. "Why is this wrapped up?"

Amy wondered what Claire would tell him.

"You nearly froze to death," Claire said.

Amy wasn't surprised by how blunt Claire was. She really liked that about her. She told it like it was. No beating around the bush with her.

He closed his eyes again.

Claire looked back at her.

"Where am I?" he asked without opening his eyes.

"In the hospital."

"How'd I get here?"

"Your wife found you outside, in the snow."

"Where is she?"

"Sherri'll be here soon. She's been here most of the time, but she went to get some sleep."

Walker closed his eyes and seemed to drift off, his breathing getting heavy and labored. Claire looked back at Amy and she shrugged. They were just about to leave the room when he jerked awake and his eyes popped open as if he had seen something horrible. "Where am I?"

Claire leaned in closer to him. "You're in the hospital. You're going to be fine. Do you remember what happened to you?"

He looked around frantically. "I don't know. This isn't right. I think I need to be somewhere else."

Amy had read that when people are agitated often touching them calms them down. She walked up to the head of his bed and put her hand on his shoulder. Claire was always encouraging her to take the lead in questioning people. Here was her chance. "The doctor said you would be fine."

He lifted his wrapped hands as if to show them to her and said, "My hands hurt. Why do my hands hurt?"

"They were severely frostbitten," Amy said, looking back at Claire.

Claire nodded at Amy, motioning for her to continue.

"Mr. Walker, you were found outside your house yesterday morning. We're trying to figure out what happened to you New Year's eve. What do you remember?"

"At night? I was at the cabin, I think."

"Yes," Amy encouraged him. "That's where you were found. You're in Durand right now."

"Oh, Durand. Okay. But why am I here?"

"Your wife found you outside in the snow and called the ambulance. They brought you here." Amy looked at Claire again. She wasn't sure how much she should tell him about his situation. Claire shook her head as if to say, give him a chance to talk, and Amy turned back to Walker.

Walker shook his head. "I don't seem to remember much about last night. Sherri wasn't there, at the cabin. I think I was by myself."

"No one else came over? It was New Year's. Did you invite someone over to celebrate with you?"

"Danielle was busy. I remember that. I don't remember anyone else coming over. I think I was alone."

"No one stopped by?" Amy asked.

He looked up at her, distress creasing his face. "I just can't remember what happened. It's like a blank. Why can't I remember?"

Amy wanted to reassure him. "The doctor said that it's not unusual to not remember much."

Claire stepped forward, patting Amy on the shoulder. "Mr. Walker, when you remember more, just let us know. We'll let you rest now, but before we go I have one final question. Who all has a key to your house besides you and Sherri?"

Walker calmed down but seemed confused when he said, "Sherri and me."

"That's all?"

He thought for a moment. "And Danielle, my daughter."

"No one else?" Amy asked. "You didn't give it to anyone else? No friends or neighbors?"

"Oh, yeah," he licked his lips. "My neighbor has a key. He was doing some work for me. John Gordon."

Amy's heart sank when she heard him say John's name. She was afraid of that. John had a key. Unfortunately she knew he also had a good reason to want Daniel Walker dead.

CHAPTER 10

2 January: 11 am

As Meg left her fourth hour class, history, she knew that Curt would be waiting for her at the lunch room. They had their routine and usually it made her happy, but today she felt like skipping lunch. She didn't want to be mad at Curt anymore, but she didn't seem to be able to let go of her anger at what he had done.

Focus on Andy, she thought. Put your anger there. He's the one who is making Curt behave this way. Plus, she wanted to find out if Curt knew anything about Bonnie's pregnancy. He certainly would have heard about it by now. News traveled the school faster than the speed of sound, if that was possible.

Curt was standing by the lunch room door, waving his brown paper bag. That gesture meant he had something good to share. His mother was a wonderful cook, old-fashioned, but wonderful. The Queen of the Bars, Curt liked to call her. Dessert bars, he would clarify.

"What do you have there?" Meg asked.

"Something you like," he teased.

"My favorite or my second favorite?"

"I get them mixed up."

"Lemon bars are my favorite, brownies are my second."

They walked into the lunchroom together and went right to their usual table. Meg tried to grab the bag, but Curt held it up high, over her head. "I think the word you're looking for is please."

She laughed, then kicked him in the ankle. When he bent over to rub the spot, she grabbed the bag and opened it. "Pumpkin walnut bars. I think they're around my fifth favorite. But still that's plenty high enough to thoroughly enjoy."

"What's on the menu?"

Meg didn't even have to look. "Olive loaf."

"When are you going to get tired of olive loaf?"

"Never. I'm fascinated by the pattern the olives make in the loaf."

"You're fascinating," Curt said and leaned over and kissed her on the nose.

"Ooo, public affection. You're trying pretty hard."

"I should have asked Mom to make lemon bars, then you'd be putty in my hands."

"Save the putty part for later."

"So you're not so mad at me anymore?" he asked hopefully.

"No, I've decided to blame it all on Andy." She laughed as she said it. Andy had always been a fairly popular guy in school. In fact when Curt and Andy had first started to hang out together, Meg was rather pleased. She sometimes felt that Curt kept to himself too much. Except for her, of course.

"That's a great idea. He has been a very bad influence on me."

They sat down and swapped halves of their sandwiches, even though Curt wasn't crazy about olive loaf. His meatloaf sandwich was on thick whole wheat bread that his mother baked. Hers was on slightly above average store-bought bread. She thought they complimented each other. She started with the meatloaf and then would move on to the olive loaf.

"Don't you wish we had a Starbucks down the street?" she asked.

"A big frappucino would sure taste good with our pumpkin bars."

"The cooks here just don't seem big into the idea of an espresso machine." Meg neatly folded up the wax paper that her sandwich had been wrapped in. She reused it as many times as she could. For the environment. "Speaking of Andy," she said, "did you hear that Bonnie Hegstrom had a baby?"

"Yeah, Kenny told me in fourth. I'm probably the last person in the whole school to know."

"Doesn't she live like in the next farm over from Andy?"

"Yeah. So what?"

"Well, do you have any idea who the dad is?"

Curt slumped back in his chair and frowned. "Geez, I haven't seen Bonnie with any guy. She rides my bus. She usually just sits with one of the other girls. You don't think that Andy…?"

Meg raised her shoulders. "He's the closest guy to her. Could have been literally just a roll in the hay."

"Boy, he's never said anything, but then we don't tend to talk much about those kind of things."

"Why don't you see what you can find out?"

Curt scrunched up his face. "Really?"

"For me?" Meg rubbed his ear lobe. She knew he just loved that. "You know, for the putty factor."

11 am

"And the cleaning lady," Amy said as she climbed into the passenger side of the squad car.

Claire had asked Amy to come back to the department with her as the floor nurse had assured her that they would let no one enter Daniel Walker's room except the nurses and doctors. His room was right across from the nurses' desk and Claire trusted them to keep a good eye on him. Plus, Walker seemed fully capable of yelling for help. By the time they left him, he was complaining about the service in the hospital. Being nearly frozen to death didn't seem to have affected his vocal chords.

Claire wanted Amy to start checking alibis. She also thought it was time to talk to Walker's lawyer and find out who got the money if he died.

The squad car turned over hard a couple times, sounding like a cow stuck in a chute, then caught and roared to life. Even through her polar-fleece gloves, Claire could feel the frigid cold radiating out of the steering wheel. "The cleaning lady, what?"

"Has a key. She let herself in while I was searching the house. I forgot to mention that. Sara Hegstrom. You know her?"

"Don't think I do."

Amy rubbed her gloved hands together. "Her husband's Clyde. They have a farm out on Goatback."

"So that makes four people with keys besides Mr. Walker: his wife, his daughter, his cleaning lady and his handyman. No butler." After scraping a small peephole through the ice on the windshield, Claire crawled out onto the street. The plows had been by but the slick surface of the roads was still treacherous.

"I guess a cleaning lady is as close as we're going to get to a butler."

"Yes, but why would the cleaning lady want to kill him?"

"Search me," Amy spoke with her head tucked turtle-like into her jacket collar. "Although maybe she was letting herself in today so that she could be the one to find him out in the snow. Clever."

"You've been reading too many Agatha Christies." Claire pulled into the government center lot. They both sat for a moment, not wanting to get out of the warm car. The sun was shining in a vivid blue sky but it looked pale and far away.

"I don't get her books. Too prim and proper for my taste. I like James Lee Burke better. Plus, there's never any snow in an Agatha Christie," Amy pointed out with satisfaction.

"Well, there's certainly no snow in a James Lee Burke book. Aren't they all set down in the bayou?"

Amy hunched her shoulders, preparing to go out into the cold. "What is a bayou anyway?"

"I think it's a slough that has never frozen over."

As they both walked into the department, Amy said, "Also, I should tell you that I think John Gordon might have a reason for wanting something bad to happen to Daniel Walker."

"John Gordon. Wasn't he Walker's handyman?"

"Yeah, he built the sauna for Mr. Walker."

"He's mad about that? What, did Walker not pay him?"

"No, it's not that. When John was gone this fall, Walker bought the family farm for a song from John's mom. She's old and not completely on top of things. Walker took advantage of her. John's pretty mad about it."

"So of the four people who had keys—two might actually want him dead."

"You know what else is weird? The cleaning lady's daughter is in the hospital too. I guess she had a baby and they didn't even know she was pregnant and she lost a lot of blood and the baby's not doing so well either."

"That is very weird." Claire wondered if these two situations could be tied together. A pregnant girl and a frozen man. "Did the girl ever clean for the Walkers?"

11:30 am

Sherri peeked her head into her husband's hospital room and could see he was sleeping. He didn't look great. They had bandaged his hands so she couldn't see the damage there, but on his face his nose had turned dark blue and he had blisters on his cheeks.

A young red-haired nurse took her arm and said, "I'm afraid no one's allowed in to see him."

"But I'm his wife."

The nurse gave her the once over and said, "Sorry. Doctor's orders."

"Why?"

"Got me."

As Sherri walked out of the room with the nurse she asked her, "When's the doctor going to be back? I'd like to speak to her."

"She said she'd stop by early afternoon. I'll let her know you'd like to talk to her. She's still quite concerned about his toes."

"He might lose them?"

"Maybe one or two. Depends on if the circulation comes back. Usually they give it a day or two."

"Thank the lord that's all he might lose."

"Yeah, he's a pretty lucky man."

Sherri had the urge to sit down on the floor and cry. She was losing Dan anyway, she wasn't sure why the thought of him dying in a snowbank made her sadder than their divorce. She just kept remembering all the good times they had had before he started in with his old ways. The trip to Paris where they had stayed in bed all day and just had meals delivered. The new car he bought her was fabulous, but looking back she realized it was the smaller gestures she treasured. Going to Stockholm Gardens for plants, him picking up a book for her when he thought she'd like it, buying her a Snickers candy bar when he learned they were her favorite.

She thought back to the beginning of their affair: the sneaking around, the sweet illicitness of it all. Now she had regrets about what she had done to Dan's first wife. Only recently had Sherri realized how awful it must have been for her.

She sat in the waiting room and wondered how long it would be before the doctor came. After reading most of the St. Paul paper, she started reading the local newspaper, staring at girls she didn't know in winter formals, boys she'd never heard of playing basketball. Just as she was wondering if she could buy a good book someplace she heard a ruckus out in the hallway.

Danielle was yelling at the same red-haired nurse. "There is no way you can keep me from seeing my father."

The nurse was standing between Danielle and Dan's hospital room. "You need to keep your voice down and go sit in the waiting room."

Danielle tried to push past the nurse, but the young woman grabbed her arm and swung her around. Sherri decided she better step in, much as she wanted nothing to do with Danielle.

"The doctor will be here soon," she said as she walked up to the two.

"What are you still doing here?" Danielle turned on her. "You're the one who shouldn't be near my father. I wouldn't be surprised if his quote accident was all your fault."

"Why would I do something like that?"

"Because of the money. That's the only reason you've ever been with my father was just to take his money. Well, it's too late now. He's done with you and even if he died, I'm the one who will get everything."

"Danielle, what are you talking about?"

"When he told me you were getting a divorce, he also told me he had already changed his will. He didn't want to take any chances with you. He left almost everything to me. I guess he should have told you that—then maybe you wouldn't have tried to kill him."

Anger welled up in Sherri, all the anger she had felt toward this bratty, mean-spirited girl for all her years with Dan. Danielle had never given her an inch, never tried to like her, never said thank you for one thing that Sherri had given her or done for her. And now this nasty girl was accusing her of trying to kill the man she had loved for so long, maybe still loved.

Her hand flew out of its own accord. With little thought, Sherri slapped Danielle across the face and said, "I would never hurt your father. Which is more than I can say for you."

Danielle shoulders shook and her eyes grew wide. A red welt sliced across her cheek. "I could sue you for that."

"Go ahead and try. I've wanted to do that for a long time. You are an ungrateful bitch."

"Better than a black widow."

CHAPTER 11

2 January: 3 pm

Ice fishing had always struck Curt as being as boring as clipping your toenails, but Andy had assured him that it was totally phat. Andy and his father had a ice-fishing house out on Lake Pepin, in small cluster of buildings close to the Pepin marina where the water was relatively shallow—around ten feet or so—and the ice was almost a foot thick.

They were sitting in Andy's dad's one-ton pickup in the parking lot of the marina, aimed out onto the ice. The day was brilliantly bright. The sun glaring off the ice made sunglasses a necessity. But the temperature was still below zero. Curt had checked the thermometer by the back door when he left the house. Up on top of the bluff it read four below.

Andy turned the truck down onto the snow-covered beach and approached the shore of the lake. There was a road carved into the snow by the vehicles that had gone out onto the ice before them. Some winters, people used this road to get across the lake and save them the time of driving forty miles to get to Lake City on the other side.

Curt didn't really like the idea of going out on the frozen lake in any kind of vehicle that weighed more than he did. He didn't mind skating on the lake, or skiing across it, but sitting in a truck moving across the ice gave him the willies. He had half a mind to open his door just in case, and he had rolled his window down, claiming he needed the air, but really wanting a quick escape route if the truck crashed through the ice.

"You're not scared, are you?" Andy asked.

"Not really," Curt said. "Did you ever see that old movie about Houdini, the one with Tony Curtis?"

"Who's Houdini?"

Sometimes Curt wondered about Andy. His scope of knowledge seemed very limited. He explained, "He was this super cool escape artist. Anyways, he has them lock him up in chains and then throw him in the Hudson River through a hole in the ice. He manages to get out of the chains, but by then the current of the river has carried him downstream, away from the hole."

"Then what?"

"Well, he finds these air pockets under the ice and breathes in them until he makes his way back up to the hole and gets out. Everyone had given him up for dead and then he appears."

"Why're you thinking about that? You don't think the truck's going to go through the ice?"

"Just reminded me."

"That Houdini sounds like that guy that froze to death and then came back to life at the hospital."

"I haven't heard about that. Was it in the paper?"

Andy shook his head. "I forget who told me about him. Weird stuff."

They were close enough to the ice houses that Curt could see the smoke coming out of a few of them. Seemed strange to go out onto the ice and then shut yourself up in a house the size of a coffin and stare at a frozen lake. But Andy had brought a deck of cards so they would have something else to do. Plus, he had brought a few beers that he had swiped from his dad's refrigerator. He claimed his dad didn't care and Curt believed him. Andy's dad seemed not to care about much except drinking beer and fiddling with machines.

Just as they got up to the nearest ice house, a crack thundered across the lake and Curt jumped. "What was that?"

"You get used to it. The ice cracks when the temperature changes. Just like wood cracks in a house when it gets really cold."

They pulled up next to an ice house and Curt stared at it. The dark structure looked like a playhouse that a goth kid would build out of leftover scraps—the shell was made out of old plywood and painted black, there were no windows, and snow was packed up a foot or so high around the bottom edges.

"Looks kinda dark," Curt said as they climbed down from the truck. "No windows?"

"That's part of the deal. You'll see," Andy said as he undid the padlock on the door and then motioned Curt to enter.

When they went inside, the small house was brighter than Curt thought it would be—light streamed up from the ice floor. Green murky light from the lake.

"This way you can see the fish. You don't want any light to get into the house. Cool, huh?"

"Yeah, way cool." Curt sat down on one of the folding chairs and stared into the water below him. Being able to see the water so clearly made him more conscious than ever that he was standing on a huge lake that at any moment could swallow him up, but he was getting used to the idea.

However, with no sun coming in, the temperature in the ice-fishing house felt even colder than outside. They were sheltered from the wind, but Curt missed the slight warmth of the sun. He pulled his cap down tighter on his head so it covered his ears and wiggled his toes around in his Sorel boots. He was wearing a long-sleeved shirt under a wool sweater under his down parka, but he was still feeling the bite of the cold.

Andy took a sledge hammer that was leaning up against the wall of the house and smashed it into a faint circular outline on the surface, re-breaking open the ice-fishing hole.

"Let's get our lines in." Andy showed Curt how to set up what he called a tip-up, a fishing line that sat on the edge of the ice hole with a flag on it that popped up if a fish took the bait. "Now we're all set. You want a brew?"

"Sure." What Curt really wanted was something warm—a steaming mug of coffee or hot chocolate—but a beer would do.

Andy handed him a bottle of Leinenkugel's, then set a couple others into a pile of ice shavings. "Gotta watch out so the brewskis don't get too cold. You heard about the guy who went out snowmobiling with a flask of brandy in his pack. He didn't know enough to keep the flask tucked into his jacket. Anyway, he's way out there, in the middle of nowhere, and he gets out the flask and takes a big swallow and freezes his whole throat. Dies from it. You know 'cuz liquor doesn't freeze at the same temperature as water."

"Yeah, I know." Curt took a swig of the beer and hoped the alcohol would warm him up. He was pretty sure that Andy's story about the snowmobiler was a rural myth. He wondered how long they'd have to be out there. He remembered what Meg wanted him to ask Andy about. "Hey, did you hear about Bonnie?"

Andy got a weird look on his face. "What about her?"

"I guess she had a baby."

Andy threw his head back. "What'd you know, a virgin birth."

"You think?" Curt asked.

"Who'd have anything to do with that little porker?"

"Oh, come on, Andy, she's not so bad."

Andy shook his head. "You won't catch me with any girl from around here. I mean, Meg's great and all, but she's about it. The chicks from the cities are way hotter. Let me tell you."

Just then the flag tipped up. Down below in the water Curt could see a shadowy form swimming in a figure eight, tail swirling through the sluggish green water. He slid down on the ice and grabbed the line and began to slowly pull the fish to the surface.

3 pm

"Okay, so what I want you to do is lift prints from any likely surface," Claire said to Bill as they both slipped on latex gloves. "Get them off all the doorknobs, the locks, the glasses."

"I know the drill," Bill said testily.

She wondered if he had a hangover. Not so unusual for the day or so after the new year, but both the foul mood and worse breath were becoming a habit with him. Since Amy and Bill had broken up, he had been drifting into some bad patterns—

often late for work, surliness, and general sloppiness in his reports. She supposed she'd have to talk to him about it, but she certainly wasn't up to it today. The way he was feeling, he just might stomp out on her and leave her to do all the work. Plus, the truth was he was better at lifting fingerprints than she was.

"I'll be wandering around, looking things over so holler if you need anything," Claire said.

Claire hadn't been in the house since they had found Daniel Walker in the snowdrift. At that time she had been so involved in getting him into the house safely and then into the ambulance that she had had no time to notice anything about the place itself. As Bill started to work, she walked the house. Mainly to see if anything caught her eye, but also to marvel at the structure.

She had heard Sherri call their house "the cabin," but it was certainly larger than what she thought of as a cabin. Maybe the conceit allowed the weekenders to think that they were building a quiet retreat in the woods, instead of a ginormous eyesore on the bluff.

As she stared at the Berber carpet, the wood-paneled walls, the stone fireplace, she had to wonder what it cost to build a place like this. She guessed at least a half a million. All that for a second home that they used for weekends mainly in the summer. Although it sounded like Walker had been living down here since he and Sherri separated.

As much as she was prejudiced against the monstrosities that were cropping up as close as they could legally get to the bluffline, she had to admit that the house was a masterpiece. Daniel Walker might be a piece of work, but he had good taste—or maybe it was Sherri who supplied that.

The fireplace was spectacular—raw chunks of limestone beautifully fitted together formed an elegant, compact surround. How wonderful it would be to sit down and light a fire and just stare into it.

But she had work to do.

She walked into the kitchen, which was obviously the heart of the house. Her churlish side came out as she wondered if they ever cooked in it. The room was outfitted, of course, with a huge, granite-slab island, a necessity in any state of the art facility. Two ovens and a microwave were built in. There was also an espresso machine, a built-in water purifier, a trash crusher, a restaurant-sized stove with six burners, and a Sub-Zero refrigerator with panels that matched the woodwork.

Rich would be in heaven. The kitchen alone probably cost more than what their whole house was worth.

Claire started pulling out drawers. The one next to the phone was usually where she found the household management stuff and sure enough a checkbook was tucked into the drawer.

Daniel Walker was meticulous. He wrote the full number of each check, carefully filling in the date written, and then to whom. She even saw the checkmarks that showed that he went through his statement and balanced his account. Figures he'd be a good businessman, he had to have made all that money somehow.

He had also written in the front page of the checkbook: expenses for cabin. So he kept a separate checkbook just for this place. Maybe it was a tax write-off. Claire slowly read through the checkbook—Excel Energy, Schaul Gas, CenturyTel, the usual bills. Then a few checks to John Gordon. Amy had mentioned that he had done work for Walker. A few checks for another neighbor—Claire guessed they were for mowing the lawn.

Then she noticed Sara Hegstrom's name and remembered that she was the cleaning lady. On an off chance, Claire counted back some months and looked through those checks. There was Bonnie Hegstrom's name. She must have cleaned for her mom in the spring.

Not quite eight months, but then Claire had heard that the baby was born premature.

Claire had told Amy that she didn't like coincidences. This one definitely needed more investigating.

3:30 pm

Amy had volunteered to talk to John Gordon about his relationship with Daniel Walker and to get the house key from him, but as she drove down the long, winding driveway to the farmhouse, she wished she had handed off the job. She hated having to sound like she was accusing John of anything. Not that she really knew him that well—he was a good ten years older than her—but she had always looked up to him.

As she was getting close to the house, a snowmobile slipped by her in the ditch, going the other way, but whoever was on it was too small to be John.

She wasn't looking forward to seeing John Gordon scowl at her. But when he answered the door, she was pleasantly surprised. He looked almost happy to see her and invited her in with some cordiality in his voice.

"What's up?" he asked as he motioned her to take a seat.

"I'm still trying to figure out what happened to Daniel Walker."

"But it was an accident, wasn't it?"

"Well, we're not sure yet. Still checking it out." She asked, "What do you think happened?"

He shrugged his shoulders. "Got me. Dan's pretty darn charming. But he's also one slippery fish. Sometimes I think these folks that come here from the cities don't get it that we're their neighbors and they're going to have to live with us for a long time. He's made some enemies. Even animals know enough not to foul their own nests."

Amy nodded. "I know what you mean."

"But as far as him weaseling the farm away from my mom, we got some good news this morning. Our lawyer called and said we might be able to wiggle out of the purchase agreement with Walker. Seems it wasn't handled the way it should have been. He said worse-case scenario we could call my mom a vulnerable adult and claim he took advantage of her. I'd hate to do that, but it's nice to have it in our back pocket in case we need to use it. But either way, it looks like we might get to keep the farm."

"That's great, John."

"Yeah, it's such a relief. I mean, I know it's not a done deal yet, but I guess I'm hopeful." He looked around. "I suppose I should offer you some coffee."

"Wouldn't say no," Amy said.

He handed her a John Deere mug and filled it to the brim. "I made the coffee so it's a little stronger than Mom's."

"Strong is good."

He sat down across from her. "How can I help you with Daniel Walker?"

"Well, we've been checking on who has keys to the house. At the moment, we're treating it like a crime scene."

"That sounds so official." He laughed, then said, "I'm sorry. Sometimes it's just hard for me to take you seriously as a cop. I mean I knew you when you were knee high to a grasshopper."

"Sometimes it's hard for me to take me seriously. But I've been doing this job for a couple years now. Even moved up in the ranks. I'm not the newbie anymore. That makes a difference." Amy asked the question she had come to ask. "Have you still got a key to Walker's house?"

"Sure. Sometimes Dan would have me go check on something for him when he wasn't here. It's always handy to have a neighbor with a key."

"Absolutely," Amy agreed.

He stood up and went to a line of hooks by the back door and pulled down a key with a piece of masking tape attached to the ring, with the name Walker written on it. "Do you want it?"

"Yeah, just for the time being. Until we figure this whole thing out." Amy heard a snowmobile pull up to the house. When she looked out the window, Edna Gordon was climbing off of it. At least, Amy guessed it was Edna under the fluorescent orange parka.

When she entered the house, Edna pushed the hood back and took off her glasses which were fogging up. Then she squinted her eyes and smiled when she saw it was Amy. "Colder than a witch's teat out there."

"And you really get the wind up here."

Edna struggled out of the parka. "Yeah, talk about your windchill factor. I don't even listen to what it is anymore. Just makes my bones ache."

She pulled a bundle of mail out of her sweater and handed the pile to John. "Nothing but bills and charities. One way or another they want your money."

"You went to get the mail on the snowmobile?" Amy asked.

"Well, I'm sure not going to walk in this weather."

"No doubt. I don't think I've been on one for a few years. Used to go out with a friend a lot when I was in high school. My dad would never get one even though I begged him to."

"You want to go for a ride?" John asked.

Amy remembered one incident where she mired the snowmobile in a huge drift and the guys she was sledding with had to come and dig her out. "I'm not that good at driving."

"I'll take you."

Amy paused. A ride through the white landscape protected behind John's broad back sounded thrilling. "I'm on duty."

"You could just say you were casing the territory."

She laughed at his attempt at cop lingo. "I guess I could."

Edna handed her the orange parka. "You need to put this on. Zip it all the way up. You got good gloves?"

Amy held out her leather choppers, then she took the parka and pulled it over her jacket. She swam in it, but she pulled the cord in the hood tight. The bottom of the parka came down to her knees, which would give her good protection from the wind. "How do I look?"

"Like a pluffy pumpkin," Edna said.

John grabbed a down vest and then put a barn jacket on over that. "We won't go out for long. Just a short spin."

The snow squeaked and crunched under their feet as they walked out to the snowmobile. A Polaris, Amy noticed, a few years old. John climbed aboard, started it and moved forward for her to climb on back. She swung her leg over the seat and found herself tucked in right behind him. She could feel the warmth of his body through his jacket.

"Stick your hands under my arms. It will protect them." He revved the motor, then gave it some gas and it grabbed the packed-down snow in the driveway and slid around. He aimed at the ditch and down they went. Then they rode straight up and out of it and onto a field on the other side.

There was a good two feet of snow on the farmlands and it made for a perfect ride on the machine. They sailed along, John gently slaloming over the open field.

Amy had forgotten how thrilling it was to snowmobile: the icy sharpness of the wind on your face, the breathless blue of the sky, the heart-opening feeling of being in another world, the buzz of the machine trailing behind.

She could tell that John had driven a snowmobile as long as he had driven a tractor, which was probably a good thirty years. Kids started on farms when they were in their early teens. While he went faster than she would have and he took sharper turns than she might have, she felt completely comfortable riding with him. He knew the land, he knew the machine, and he wasn't particularly a risk taker.

At least she hoped he wasn't. She prayed he had nothing to do with what had happened to Daniel Walker.

CHAPTER 12

2 January: 4:30 pm

Yup, we're finally doing it." Claire had been meaning to tell her sister Bridget about her upcoming wedding, but had been so busy that she finally had to grab a moment at work and call her at the pharmacy. The office had cleared out so there wasn't anyone to overhear her conversation.

"Well, it's about time. This calls for a celebration. When are you planning for the big event—in June?"

"No, Valentine's Day. And I don't want it to be so big. "

"What? But that's only a month and a half away."

"We're going to have a small ceremony and then maybe a nice dinner afterwards."

"That's all?"

"Hey, Rich is over fifty. We've both already been married once. I don't need to wear the big white dress again. I know he's just doing it so he can get my pension."

Bridget started laughing. "So you asked him."

"I figured it was my turn."

"You two are wild. Let me know what I can do." Bridget paused for a second, then said, "Well, I might have a date."

"Great. Who?"

"A doctor."

"Terrific. Maybe he'll be as smart as you."

"He's younger than me."

"Good. How much younger?"

"Only three years. He's from India."

"Wonderful. What's his name?"

"Satish."

"I can't wait to meet him. Let's make it before the wedding. We'll have you over for dinner."

"We've only been out on a couple dates, but I feel like I've known him a long time. He's very sweet and he has such good manners. I'll tell you more later. I gotta get back to work."

"Me too. Hey, before you go, is it possible for a woman to get pregnant and go to term and not know that she's pregnant?"

"I've heard of it happening. A big woman who just figures she's putting on weight. A friend of a friend went in to the doctor because she thought she had a tumor growing in her belly. Turned out she was eight months pregnant. Why?"

"A girl at Meg's school just had a baby in her bed. Claimed she didn't even know she was pregnant."

"Sounds like an easy way to do it."

"Come over some time. Bring that child of yours."

"Will do."

When Claire looked up, Sherri Walker was standing at the front desk of the sheriff's department. Claire almost didn't recognize the woman—she was wearing her hair up in a ponytail and had wire-rimmed glasses on. She looked drawn and tired. As Claire walked over to her, she also saw that Sherri had little if no make-up on and was wearing the same clothes as yesterday.

She obviously hadn't come prepared to spend the night, which told Claire a bit more about her relationship with her estranged husband.

"Thanks for coming down," Claire said.

"Feels good to get out of that hospital."

"Let's go someplace where we can talk privately." Claire led the way to a small conference room. All that was in the room was a table and four chairs. No windows to the outside, no posters on the walls. A bright overhead light glared down on them.

"It sounds like your husband is doing much better today."

"Yes, it's quite a relief. I still can't believe he's going to make it." Sherri sounded genuinely pleased.

"I need to ask you a few questions."

"Yes, anything I can do to help you find out who did this to Dan."

"Mrs. Walker, we can't be sure that anyone else is involved. We have no evidence that anyone else was at the house with Mr. Walker and just your word for it that the door was locked."

"But it was locked," Sherri insisted.

"You think it was—but maybe it was just jammed."

"No, I had to flip the deadbolt."

"In that case there is a very slight chance that your husband locked the door behind himself and then lost the key."

"That sounds ridiculous."

Claire had to admit it did. "What do you think happened?"

"I'm beginning to think that Danielle might have been behind it."

"Why?"

"Well, I just learned from her today that if Dan died, then she stood to inherit most everything."

"This was news to you?"

"Yes, she claimed that when Dan and I separated, he changed his will and made her the sole beneficiary. It does sound like something he would do. Dan likes to believe he and Danielle are so close but she is very headstrong and independent. She's used to getting her way with him. If she wanted some money and he wouldn't give it to her I could see her trying something like this."

"You think she would kill her dad?"

"No, I think she would get someone else to do it."

"She says she was out with friends for New Year's Eve, but I will check into that." Claire looked at her notebook. "I also wanted to ask you about your cleaning lady."

"Sara Hegstrom? Why?"

"Well, I was just wondering who pays her?"

"I used to, I suppose Dan does now."

"Does Bonnie Hegstrom clean for you too?"

"She's filled in for her mom a few times. I don't think she does as good a job, but I figure she's got to learn somehow."

"So if Dan paid Bonnie for a cleaning in the spring, then that would mean that you weren't there?"

"I don't get why you're asking these questions."

"I'll explain in a moment. Would he only have paid her if you weren't there?"

"Yes, that's most likely."

"Why are you and your husband separated?"

Sherri tilted her head back and tears filled her eyes. She dabbed at them and Claire gave her a Kleenex. "A couple times

I came down to the cabin and found long dark hairs in the bed. I obviously don't have dark hair and Dan barely has hair. I tried to let it go but things were not going well between us anyways. One night I blew up and just stormed out."

She paused for a moment, drawing in a deep breath. "I thought he'd come after me. I thought he loved me. But he didn't. A few weeks later when we finally talked, he admitted he had been sleeping with other women, but he said they weren't important, he said the marriage just wasn't doing it for him. A while later he did ask me to come back, but by then I was seeing more clearly how unhappy I had been in our life." She rubbed her hands on her face. "You know, I do love him, but I just don't want to go through that again. It's too awful."

"Would it surprise you if one of the women he had been sleeping with was Bonnie Hegstrom?"

Sherri cocked her head to one side. "Bonnie? Little Bonnie? But she's just a kid, still in high school."

"Well, that little girl just had a baby. And she was working at your house about nine months earlier. I was just wondering what you know about that."

"Nothing," Sherri started laughing and then it turned to tears again. "Oh, that poor girl. I don't know. She's certainly not Dan's type. He likes them long-legged and sassy. I should know—he started going out with me while he was still married. Not how I would describe Bonnie. But she was available. I suppose it's possible. What did she have—a boy or a girl?"

"A little boy."

5 pm

Amy found Sara Hegstrom standing next to a crib in the nursery, staring down at a mewling baby.

"Is that your new grandchild?"

"Yes, and he doesn't even have a name yet. Isn't that awful?"

Amy didn't think it was so awful, but nodded. "I should have asked you before when I saw you at the Walker house, but I need to have your key to their house. Do you have it with you?"

Sara turned and looked at her. "Why in heaven's name? Don't they trust me to clean their house anymore?"

"No, it's not that. Really almost a formality. But we're not sure what happened to Mr. Walker and we're treating the house like a crime scene."

Sara rummaged in her purse. "I need that job. Money's really tight right now. With the economy sinking fast. The price of feed has sky rocketed, but we're not getting any more for our milk."

"I'm sure they'll want you to keep cleaning. Especially when we're done with the place."

"I've always wondered about that. Do you just turn everything upside down and leave it?"

"No, we're pretty careful, but there will be some powder residue left from lifting fingerprints. Speaking of which, we'll need to get your prints."

Sara looked alarmed.

"Just to eliminate them," Amy assured her.

"Is he going to be all right?"

"It looks like it. He might lose a few phalanges, but that's all."

"Phalanges. I haven't heard that word since high school health. After what he's been through that's not much to lose, but then Daniel Walker was always a lucky man."

"What do you mean?"

"Just all his money, that beautiful home, his lovely wife. He's got a lot to be envied for."

Amy nodded toward the baby. "Sara, do you have any idea who the father is?"

"What's that got to do with anything?"

"We're just checking all possibilities and Bonnie did clean for the Walkers a few times."

Sara's eyes opened wide. "You think him? Oh, my lord."

"Just wondering."

"Bonnie hasn't told me who. I did ask her once, but she just turned to face the wall. I haven't wanted to push her about it much as I want to know. In a way I really don't care. We've got to deal with getting them both out of the hospital.

"Can we walk down to her room together and see what she has to say?"

"I guess so," Sara said reluctantly.

When they came to Bonnie's room, she was sleeping. A large girl with long, faded brown hair which fanned around her face. Her mouth was cracked and a slow steady breath came out of her. A plain girl with large hands. She had always struck Amy as a good farm girl. But now she saw, in her own quiet way, that Bonnie had a kind of beauty about her.

"Don't wake her up, please," Sara said.

"No. It can wait."

6:30 pm

Nothing was open along the river in the winter—no coffee-shops, no antique stores, not even the pizza place—and it was too cold to sit in a car and park so Meg and Curt were sprawled in her living room with their legs crossed over each other. There was no rule saying they couldn't be alone in Meg's room, but Meg knew from experience that either Rich or Claire were liable to knock on the door at any time and then walk in. No privacy there. They might as well sit right out in the open.

"I swear the fish was this big," Curt held his hands out stretched wide apart. "It was three feet long if it was an inch. I wish you could have seen it. I wish I could have carried it back for you and fed the whole family with it."

"No way," Meg laughed at him.

"Way way," he argued. "I could see it through the ice. Meg, it's so cool to sit in darkness and be able to see the fish moving below you. Creepy and cool at the same time."

"So now are you going to be an ice-fisherman, too, besides just a super-duper hero?"

"Knock it off with the superhero."

She could tell he was getting a little exasperated with her. "Hey, I'm not the one who calls you Mega-turkey or whatever your name is."

Curt cocked his head and stared at her. "I think I'm starting to figure out what's going on with you. You're jealous. I do believe you're jealous of Andy."

"Why would I be jealous of that turdball?"

"Because I have fun with him. Even if he is a bit of a turdball. I thought you wanted me to have some guy friends."

Meg remembered she had suggested something like that a few months ago. "Well, yeah, but smart ones, not goonballs who just want to sit in the dark and spear fish or kill troglodytes."

"You are so jealous." Curt got on his knees and poked her in the side.

"No pokes," she said. "Or I'll have to get mad at you again."

"You deserve a few pokes for being such a ninny."

She pulled him toward her and he wrapped his arms around her. "What do you deserve?" she asked. "Did you find out anything from Mr. Andy about Bonnie?"

"As a matter of fact," Curt whispered into her neck, then gently nipped it. "I did ask him."

Meg pushed him away so she could see his face and hear him better. "What? Tell me."

"Beg." He took her face in his hands, laughing at her.

"Please, my little honey pot, please."

"All right. Since you asked so nicely. No." Then he claimed a kiss.

Meg sputtered. "What? That's all?"

"Yup. Andy was disgusted when I even suggested it and then went on to say that girls from the cities are much hotter."

"How would he know?"

"I guess he hooked up with a girl whose family owns one of those big houses on the bluff this fall."

"So he says," Meg said. "Do you believe him?"

"Kinda. What I'm more surprised about is that he isn't bragging about it more often. It's not like him to keep quiet about something."

"You're right. Something's weird here with Mr. Andy. I think you have more sleuthing to do," she said as she leaned into him for a more significant kiss.

CHAPTER 13

3 January: 7 am

Claire knew the doctors started rounds early at the hospital so she decided to go straight there before work and see if she could catch Dr. Cornwall and get the scoop on Daniel Walker.

Before going outside, she looked out the kitchen window and checked the thermometer. The temperature had hit a high of zero. A slight warm-up. She piled into her full-length down coat and pulled on her hat with the ear-flaps. Then she pushed the button on her remote to start the squad car—a Christmas present from Rich. If she waited a few minutes the car might almost be warm before she started driving. It seemed to make her whole day go better if she didn't have to start it shivering in a frigid vehicle.

Watching out for black ice on the frozen roads, Claire made it to the hospital by seven. As she was walking up to Daniel Walker's room, she saw Dr. Cornwall turning a corner down at the end of the hall. She jogged to catch up with her.

"May I talk to you for a moment?"

"Sure, it's actually a slow day for me." Dr. Cornwall smiled and swept back her ponytail. "Winter doldrums I guess. No one wants to see a doctor until they pay for their Christmas presents."

"I never thought of that. I just wanted to check on Daniel Walker. How's he doing?"

"Well, except for the fact that he's going to lose three toes on his left foot, quite well."

"Does he seem with it to you?"

"Yes, surprisingly so. His mental facilities seem to be intact. Neurologically he's sound."

"Is he remembering what happened?"

"From what I can gather, not completely. I haven't questioned him much about the incident. However, he knows what year it is, he knows where he is, and he doesn't want to lose his toes. All that seems pretty normal to me."

"How much longer will you keep him in the hospital?"

"I'd say he'll leave in the next day or two, depending on how the amputations go."

Somehow hearing the word, "amputation," and realizing that the surgery was going to happen soon, put a darker spin on losing a few toes. "What will that do to him—having his toes cut off?"

"His balance might be affected. We don't realize how much we rely on our toes to keep us from pitching forward when we walk and stand. And he'll be in some pain. But other than that, he should be fine. While he looks awful, the rest of his frostbite patches are healing nicely. He's lucky he's not going to lose his nose."

The thought of losing a nose made Claire's stomach turn. "Yeah," she agreed. "I'm curious. How long could he have stayed at that temperature and still been able to be resuscitated?"

"That's hard to say."

Claire wondered why so much was hard for a doctor to say. Maybe that was a phrase they learned in school and were taught to preface most sentences with it. "Give it your best shot."

"There are too many variables. I've heard of someone being revived after being out in the cold for over a day. But that guy was at least wearing clothes. Outside like that, I wouldn't have thought much longer than he did. Mr. Walker was about as close to dying as one can get."

10 am

Danielle's cellphone buzzed in her pocket. The hospital had a thing about cell phones. They freaked out if they rang so she had to put hers on vibrate. She took the phone out and read the message: "mt me B K PLZ DM."

"Danger Man." What a punk Andy was. She looked around the dingy waiting room. But she wouldn't mind getting out of there. She didn't know anyone else around this craphole little town. It would be nice to talk to someone about how weird this all was. Burger King was as good a place as any and at least she might get some regular food. The slop in the hospital cafeteria sucked.

They still weren't letting anyone but the cops in to see her father, but she slipped by his room as she was leaving and waved at him. He was sleeping, but at least she had tried. His face looked so terrible it gave her the heaves.

When she got down to the main floor she asked directions to the Burger King and then bundled up to go out the door. Thank goodness none of her friends could see her. Sherri had lent her a down coat and she looked like the Michelin Man. But at least it kept her somewhat warm. Her car wasn't too cold inside; the sun had warmed it up.

When Danielle got to the Burger King, she parked as close to the door as she could and looked at herself in the mirror. Was it even worth it to put on lipstick? She pulled her tube out and it would hardly even slide across her lips. Why was she bothering for Andy anyway? She hoped he didn't think there was still something going on between them, if so she'd have to set him straight.

It hadn't really worked out on any level. He was overly anxious and didn't know how to take his time. Plus, he was way too young for her. She wanted to play around for a few more years, but then she wanted to find someone like her dad, someone who knew how to make money and, even more importantly, knew how to spend it on her.

When she walked into the joint, he was already there, waving at her from a booth. Waving at her. What was that about? She pointed at the counter and he held up a bag of food. She ordered a cheeseburger and small fries, then she splurged on a shake. She figured she needed the extra calories to keep warm. She heard you burned off lots of calories shivering.

When Danielle slid into the booth across from Andy, he ducked his head, then said, "Hey."

"Hey, yourself, farmer," she said. He hated it when she rubbed it in that he lived on a farm.

"Pretty cold, huh?"

"I don't want to talk about the weather. It is what it is." She bit into her hamburger and tasted the tang of the ketchup.

"Yeah, I guess." Andy slurped at his soft drink. "How's it going with your dad? How's Sherri handling it?"

She tried not to snap at him. "He's doing okay. Don't even say Sherri's name to me. She's a bitch."

Farm Boy laughed. "And you're not?"

She flinched and felt herself close to slapping him, but she had to play it cool, not let him know she had her own vulnerabilities. "What's with you? This has been really hard on me. And she doesn't help matters at all."

He sat back. "Well, I know you're busy, but you could at least give me a call from time to time."

Man, he was like a little pussy, so needy, but then that was why she had picked him out at the beach—easy to handle. That and his bod. Plus, he had amused her with his hick ways. There were so many things he didn't know and he was just so excited to find them out. It had been kinda fun. But now he was a drag.

"Listen, I need to focus right now. Focus on my dad. Let me just get through this and I'll give you a call."

"What's going to happen with your dad? Do you think he and Sherri are going to get back together again?"

"Over my dead body. What a horrible thought. I sincerely hope not. In fact, I will do everything in my power to see that that doesn't happen."

●　●　●

3 pm

"They're gone," Daniel said as he stared down at the foot of his bed.

Sherri sat down in the only chair in the bare room. A blond-haired nurse stood in the doorway.

"I know," she said, looking down at the lump in the bed which was his bandaged foot.

"They took off three of my toes and part of my foot."

"I'm sorry, Dan."

He shrugged. "I can't feel a thing. What's a couple toes?" He looked up at her. "But my nose itches."

"Don't start scratching it now. You don't want to get it infected."

"Where have you been?" he asked.

"Out in the waiting room. I'm not allowed to be with you alone," she explained to him.

"Why not?" he asked, a slight whine in his voice.

Sherri forced herself to look at him. His face looked even more awful than it had yesterday. The blisters were weeping and his nose was a dark, stormy blue. Only his eyes looked like they used to—deep brown and steady. Daniel had been a handsome man when she first met him. He had aged a bit since then—silver streaks in his remaining hair, a bit of a paunch, but not bad. But the way he looked now, he could star in a horror film.

"Because the cops think I might have tried to kill you." Sherri figured there was no sense in keeping it a secret from him.

He gave a raw laugh that sounded like something had scraped his throat. "That's ridiculous. Why would you want to kill me?"

"For your money."

"Would you kill me for my money?"

"No, it doesn't matter that much to me. Plus, Danielle just informed me that you had changed your will and I wouldn't have gotten any anyway."

"Danielle told you that? She's been busy. Don't believe everything she says." He laughed, which turned into a throaty cough. The he spit out, "Anyway, you're too lazy and too nervous to try to kill me."

"That's true too." Sherri found herself smiling, in spite of his nasty comment. Daniel Walker did know her quite well. After all, they had worked together for ten years and then been married for the last five. He should know her.

"When am I going to get to go home? I keep asking them and no one will tell me. Can you find out?"

Sherri looked at the nurse. "Do you know?"

"Might be as soon as tomorrow," the nurse answered.

"You don't have to stand there. I'm not worried about Sherri. She's still my wife," Daniel said to the nurse. He was always trying to boss everyone around. Sherri wondered what the nurse would say.

The blond-haired nurse smiled and said, "I do have to be here. It's part of my job."

Daniel waved his hand. "Don't you have something better to do? People's lives to save?"

"Not at the moment."

"Well, it's your time. I guess you can do what you want with it." Daniel turned back to Sherri. "Any chance you could get me something decent to eat? I'm starving to death here."

"What would you like?"

"What I'd really like is a steak, but I guess a hamburger would do. With the whole works—fries and all. Cholesterol be damned."

"I'll get you a hamburger for dinner."

He leaned his head back. His eyes closed. He sighed, then opened his eyes and said, "Sherri, thank you for being here."

She blinked her eyes. She did not want him to see her cry for many reasons—her pride and his pride too. But he hadn't spoken so kindly to her in a long time. "You're welcome."

CHAPTER 14

3 January: 3:30 pm

Claire was surprised to walk into Bonnie's room and find her alone in bed with the bundle of a baby tucked in next to her. In front of the young girl was a tray of food—soup, bread, chocolate milk. Lots of liquids. She must be trying to breastfeed. This had to be a good sign.

Bonnie was staring down at her newborn, touching him on the face as if seeing if he were real. Her long brown hair hung like a shawl around her shoulders and she looked like a plump Madonna.

"Bonnie," Claire asked. "How're you doing?"

Bonnie started, then looked up and saw the uniform and held her baby tighter. "Who are you?"

"A deputy sheriff, Meg Watkins' mom. I didn't mean to startle you, but I'd like to ask you a few questions. Everything is fine." Claire stepped closer and couldn't help but lean down to admire the baby. He had a broad face with faint, wide eyebrows and a chubby hand was near his mouth, waving around. His hair was thick but very light, appearing like down on his head. She had the nearly irresistible urge to reach out and stroke him, but she needed to ask Bonnie a few questions first. "He's adorable."

"Do you think so? I think he's kinda scrawny and squished looking."

"But look at that hair. He's going to chunk out soon enough, but don't worry if he drops a little right at first. That's normal."

Claire pulled up a chair and sat down next to the girl. "You can keep eating. I just wanted to ask you a few things."

"About what?" Bonnie spooned up some soup.

"I'll be really straight with you. I'm wondering about your relationship to Daniel Walker."

The spoon Bonnie had been holding clanged to the tray, then fell to the floor.

"I'll get it," Claire said, not wanting the girl to try to reach down from the bed and also to give her a second to gather herself together. When she handed the spoon back to Bonnie, she caught her eyes and said, "This is just between you and me. No one else will know."

"Why are you asking me about Mr. Walker? I just did some house cleaning work for him."

"What do you think of him?"

Bonnie shrugged. "He's a nice guy. Pretty smart."

"Does he pay you well?"

"Better than I could get any other place around here."

Claire had been thinking about how she would phrase the important question. She knew many interrogators came at things slantwise, but she tended to come at the issue straight ahead, especially with someone like Bonnie. The young girl would be unprepared for it and since she was probably not much of a liar, be forced to come out with something that was close to the truth.

"Bonnie, who is the father of your baby?"

Bonnie lifted her head like a doe hearing a noise that might mean danger. She looked around the room.

"This is between you and me," Claire assured her.

"Do you really need to know?"

"It might be helpful."

"I think you already know."

"Do I?"

"Well, you asked me about Mr. Walker."

Claire noticed that Bonnie called him Mister. They must not have gotten very close. "Was it just once?"

Bonnie shook her head.

"More than that?"

"Only twice. My mom was sick so I went and cleaned their house. Mr. Walker was there both times."

"Did he force you?"

Bonnie shook her head again. "No, not really. He was very nice to me. We sat and talked and he even gave me a beer. Just one beer. But it wasn't like I was drunk or anything. You know, we were just hanging out. He treated me like an adult. He asked me questions about myself. He wasn't a lech or anything. I don't know. It just happened. I didn't mind. It was kinda nice."

"Are you sure? You know what he did was against the law, because of your age."

"Really? That seems stupid, when I went along with it. In a way, I was glad to get the first time over with. Everyone makes such a big deal about it."

Claire nodded. Thank goodness he hadn't forced her. But he had sure left her holding the package, so to speak.

"And you really didn't know you were pregnant?"

"No. My stomach hurt, but I just figured it was cause I was gaining weight. I was embarrassed about that."

"What about your period?"

"It's always been a little irregular. I never paid much attention to it."

"So Mr. Walker doesn't know he's a father?"

Bonnie looked down and shook her head.

"Do you want him to know?" Claire asked.

Bonnie shrugged.

"Let me be clear. Mr. Walker broke the law. We could arrest him for what he did to you."

Bonnie looked up. "Do you have to? I'd rather keep it quiet. Does he even have to know?"

"I think he should know. At least he needs to take responsibility for his actions."

"So are you going to arrest him?"

Claire thought of Daniel Walker, frozen and blistering, having parts of his body cut off. Bonnie probably wasn't even aware of what had happened to him, that he was on the next floor of the hospital. "We'll see."

The baby started fussing, his broad face turning red. When Bonnie cuddled him, he quieted. She seemed to know what to do with him already.

"Have you named him yet?"

"No. I've been watching him, trying to see what he looks like to me. I've thought of Kevin and Logan. What do you think?"

"Those both sound like very good names. Solid. Just like your beautiful baby is going to be."

"Thanks."

"Bonnie, I need to ask you one more question. Does anyone know about your relationship with Mr. Walker? Your parents? His wife?"

"Not my mom. Just my dad."

"What'd he say when he found out?"

"That he was going to kill him."

4 pm

John Gordon stared out the window at the brittle sun glaring off the icy crust on top of the snow. He didn't know what to do with himself. He felt like he was frozen inside and it wasn't just because of the weather. He was waiting to hear back from the lawyer, trying to decide what he would do depending on which way the phone call went.

No matter what happened with the farm, he didn't feel like he could leave his mother again, but there was no work for him to do in Pepin County during the winter.

He'd put in an application at the dog food factory and at the cabinet maker down near Hager City, but he wasn't holding his breath. Both places had told him they weren't hiring, but still let him fill out an application.

Until he knew what was going to happen with the farm, he felt all tied up in knots. The thought of losing the homeplace made him sick, like the earth had changed into a land he didn't know anymore. How could something like this have happened to him? He had planned on spending his whole life on the farm. It was the only place he felt real.

There were projects to do around the house and out in the barn, but he didn't feel like doing anything to make the place any better if Walker was going to buy it. John was pretty sure that Walker had no intention of fixing up the house. He'd tear it down, cut up the land and sell it off to some rich folks for tennis courts and swimming pools. Good farmland going to waste. Where did people think food was going to come from in the future if they kept on developing all the land that way?

He could really kick himself. He should have put the farm in a trust with the Western Wisconsin Land Trust when he had the chance. But now it might be way too late.

Slamming his hand against the glass, he decided he couldn't stay in the house any longer. His mother was upstairs taking a nap. He noticed she was taking one most days now. She definitely seemed to be running low on energy. He wondered when she had been in to the doctor. Might be time for a check-up. He wasn't looking forward to the day when he would lose her too.

As he pulled on his down jacket, he decided he didn't need to tell her he was going out. He wouldn't be gone long.

Deputy Sheriff Amy hadn't been by in the last day. He got such a kick out of her being a cop. She looked about as cute as they come in her uniform. He wondered what she looked like out of it. He remembered her vaguely from just seeing her around—at the grocery store with her mom, at the beach, at the Fort playing pool. She had been a funny looking girl, short and chunky, but she had slimmed down some and filled out nicely. Plus, she had always had a great smile. Like a light came on in her eyes and it was catchy. Infectious, he guessed was the word that might describe that quality.

Just as he was all bundled up the phone rang. When he answered he heard Dean Lloyd on the other end, the lawyer.

"Cold enough for you?" Dean asked.

"No, I like it so my eyeballs freeze when I step outside."

Dean gave a guffaw. "Hey, buddy, I don't have great news."

"Shoot."

"Well, as far as I can tell, this contract seems pretty solid. I don't see any way out of it as it stands. We might need to talk about that other way of trying to get out of the contract."

John knew he meant declaring his mother incompetent. "Let me think on it. I'll give you a call tomorrow."

"Sure. I'm around. Unless I can find a cheap fare to Cancun."

John gave a dry laugh and signed off.

He stepped out into the frigid day and felt his shoulders rise to ward off the cold. An instinctive movement all winter long. Exhausting. As he walked toward the barn, the snow squeaked beneath his boots, sounding like mice caught in a trap. He had always wondered if it were possible to tell the temperature by the sound the snow made. Maybe someone had studied that, some smart scientist.

He had wanted to be a scientist when he was a kid. He had loved experiments and figuring out how things worked, but his mom had needed him on the farm when it came time for him to consider college. So that put an end to that. Now at forty, he was too old to even think about doing anything but fix tractors and measure out feed and plant corn. He was just a farmer, that's all he'd ever be, but it was enough.

He decided he would walk down the quarter mile driveway and see if the mail had come. He got such a kick out of his mom driving the snowmobile down to get it, but it made good sense. Last thing she needed to do at her age was fall on the ice. Especially when she was all by herself. Another thing he hated to think about, but he knew his sister checked in on her frequently and called her every day.

John loved the flow of the land. In winter the contours really stood out, the swales and mounds, the curve of it all. Like looking at a woman lounging naked in bed, her white skin glistening and you just wanted to run your hand down it. He was in love with this place, had been all his life. He'd do almost anything to keep it.

7 pm

"So what do you hear through the school grapevine about Bonnie's pregnancy?" Claire asked Meg, who was sprawled on the couch, watching "American Idol."

"Mom, sh-sh-sh. It's right down to the finals and he's just about to sing."

Claire sat down and watched the TV with her daughter. A tall, dark-haired man who looked like a cross between Elvis and Liberace, stood stock still on stage and sang an amazing version of "Ring of Fire."

When he was done singing, Claire turned to Meg and said, "Wow."

"Yeah, he's great, but he's not going to win."

"How can you be so sure?"

"Too weird. A little too dark and scary for teeny-boppers."

"Aren't you a teeny-bopper?"

"No way. I'm much more sophisticated than that." Meg sat up. "What'd you want to know about Bonnie? How did you hear about her baby?"

Claire didn't want Meg to know why she was asking. She tried to keep her job out of her home life if she could. It was not always possible in this small community. Not so long ago Meg had been right in the middle of a case, but had come through it all with surprisingly little trauma. Or at least nothing evident at the moment. "Just saw her at the hospital and wondered what had happened there. I heard she didn't even know she was pregnant."

"Can you believe it? It's like one of those urban myths—girl delivers baby in bed—but then it's really happening to this person you know. Too strange. Everybody was talking about it."

"What are kids saying at school?"

"Everybody's like wow, how'd that go down. I mean she's never even gone out with anyone. Nobody could even believe that she had had sex."

"So no one was guessing who the father was?"

"Not a clue."

Claire slid down next to her daughter. "How're you and Curt?"

"Oh, you hear the word sex and then you want to know how we are?"

"Now, don't get so defensive."

Meg laughed. "Okay, I guess. He's been hanging with this one guy I don't really like very much. But other than that, things are fine."

"What guy?"

"Andy Palmquist."

Rich walked into the room and plopped down in his chair. "What're you two gossiping about?"

"This and that," Meg said. "Nothing you'd be interested in."

"Well, speaking of Andy, I just saw him today at lunch. Kinda surprised he wasn't at school."

"The seniors can leave if they want. A perk."

"Where'd you have lunch?" Claire asked.

"At Burger King. I was in Durand picking up some stuff at the Co-op. Yeah, Andy was sitting there with Danielle Walker."

Claire pushed herself up. "Danielle Walker? Really? How do you know who she is?"

"She and her dad came and got some pheasant from me for Thanksgiving this year. She's pretty memorable."

Claire and Meg looked at each other. Almost in unison they said, "Andy and Danielle?"

Claire asked, "What would they be doing together?"

Rich said, "He probably met her down here. What's so surprising about that?"

Meg said, "Why would someone like Danielle go out with Andy? When she would come down to the beach, she wouldn't give any of us locals the time of day."

"I wonder," Claire said.

CHAPTER 15

4 January: 10 am

I'm getting out today," Daniel Walker said to Claire as she walked in his hospital room. He was sitting on the edge of his bed, one of his feet bandaged, the other bare but blistered.

Claire stood next to his bed and said, "Congratulations." She was surprised to notice that he looked a little better than he had yesterday—his face had more color and he seemed more lively. His face was still a scabbed-over, blistering mess, but he was even smiling.

"Can I go back to the cabin?" He looked up at her. "Or is it still under your jurisdiction? Casing the joint?"

"We're done checking it out. You can stay there. I have to tell you, so far we've found no particular evidence of anyone else in the house with you that night. All the fingerprints checked out—no surprises. Are you remembering anything more about what happened?"

"I've tried. I think back and I can vaguely remember being in the sauna, I can remember having a cigar, and then it just goes blank. Like a curtain falls down in my brain. But I'm not worried about going back to the house. To tell you the truth, I don't think anyone did this to me. I know you think someone tried to do this to me, but I'm not so sure. I have a feeling I decided to go out and roll in the snow and just couldn't get back in." Walker shrugged his shoulders. "After all, I was doing some drinking."

"But Sherri claims that all the doors were locked."

Walker looked at the door as if checking to see if anyone was there, then back to Claire. "Just between you and me, she has a vivid imagination. She probably had trouble getting the back door open and decided it had been locked. I wouldn't trust her memory. Anyway, she's going to come and stay with me for a few days while I recuperate so I won't be alone."

Claire stepped closer and lowered her voice. "There's something else I need to talk to you about, Mr. Walker. I'm not sure that you are aware of this but Bonnie Hegstrom is in the hospital too and she just had a baby."

His head jerked up, but his voice was casual. "Bonnie. Sure, I know Bonnie. Cute kid."

"Yes, well, she told me that you are probably the father of this baby."

He braced himself with both arms and stared at her. "What? You've gotta be kidding me. She's lying if she said that."

"Mr. Walker. I think you need to think about what you're saying. We can do a paternity test if it comes to that. She's claiming that you had sex with her twice when she was working for you."

His voice deepened as he explained, "It wasn't like that. We were just fooling around. I didn't force her or anything."

"She's not saying you did, but, you know, Bonnie's underage."

It was hard for Claire to read Walker's face, but he shook his head. "No, I didn't know. How old is she?"

"Only seventeen."

He sagged down onto the bed, his arms giving way and his head dropping to his chest. "I had no idea. She's a big girl. I didn't really think about it. I was sure she was at least nineteen or twenty. I didn't know."

"Unfortunately not knowing is no excuse."

"Are you going to put me in jail?" He looked down at his red, scabby hands. "Like this?"

"I have to talk to her parents. Nobody's pressing charges at the moment, so you're free to go home. But don't think about leaving the state."

"To tell you the truth, I was thinking of going to Arizona and bake in the sun for the rest of the winter."

"You hang tight and watch your back."

"Hey, I don't have any enemies."

Claire didn't bother to list for him the ones she could think of off hand.

11 am

As Amy walked into the Government Center, she knew she had huge red roses blooming on her cheeks. The cold always did that to her. She stripped off her jacket, her scarf and her gloves, and was glad that she had pulled office duty for the next few hours. She had just spent the first half of the day tagging stranded cars and helping people who didn't have enough sense to wear some warm clothes get home.

She jumped up and down and jogged to her desk just to get the blood circulating in her body. Once the cold got into your skin, it was hard to ever get warm again.

"You got a moment? I'd like to put our heads together about what's going on with Mr. Walker," Claire said, coming up to Amy with two coffees in her hands. "He's getting out of the hospital and doesn't seem to feel he has anything to worry about. I'm not so convinced."

Amy happily took the mug of coffee and held it in her cold hands. "Conference room?"

"Sure, I always like to write on the chalkboard in there. It seems to help me organize my thoughts," Claire said as they walked to the conference room. "I have a couple things to tell you. You know Bonnie Hegstrom?"

"Yeah, she just had a baby. Poor kid. There goes her life."

"Well, I had a talk with her and she claims Daniel Walker is the father."

"Shit," Amy said and spilled some of the coffee on the table. "Excuse my language. That just popped out."

"Hey, I hear you. There are too many coincidences happening with this case."

Claire wrote DANIEL WALKER on the board. "Then I go to see Walker today—and as I'm leaving he says to me, 'But I don't have any enemies.'"

Amy laughed. "That's a good one. I think the better question is—does he have any friends?"

"Oh, lord, I know. Well, at least his wife and him seem to be getting along better. Sherri is going to go home and stay with him while he recoups."

Claire wrote SHERRI WALKER below the first name. "She's gotta be a suspect. The dumped wife. It's a cliché, but then that's why such things are clichés—because they happen all the time. Plus, I still think she's got the best motive."

Amy nodded. "Money."

"Love and money." Claire looked at the board, then wrote: CLYDE HEGSTROM, REVENGE. "Bonnie told me that her father knew about Daniel Walker being the father of her baby. She claims he said he was going to kill Walker. I don't think she knew that he was in the hospital with her."

"What about his wife, Sara, the cleaning lady?"

"Well, from what I can gather, she didn't leave the hospital once the baby was born. She was there when Walker was brought in. She slept right next to her daughter's bed, according to the nurses."

Amy knew she was going to have to add a name to the list. Reluctantly, she said, "I think you need to write down John Gordon."

"Really?"

"Yeah, he was pretty darn angry about Mr. Walker trying to buy the farm from his mother. I don't blame him. Walker really took advantage of his mother."

Claire wrote: JOHN GORDON. Then she wrote: MO-TIVE: FARM, REVENGE

"I suppose it could have been someone from the Cities, but it's a long way to come on such a cold night."

Amy thought of one more person. "What about his daughter, Danielle?"

"I'll add her to the list, but she seems to be very close to her father. She's hardly left the hospital."

"Well, according to her, she was really the one who was going to inherit all his money. She was throwing this in Sherri's face during one of their fights. I checked with the lawyer and it's true. As of New Year's Eve, she stood to gain the most from Walker's death. Plus, she gives me the creeps."

"Well, that alone is a pretty good reason." Claire wrote: DANIELLE WALKER. Then added, MOTIVE: MONEY

2:30 pm

Meg caught Andy as he was leaving school. She grabbed his arm and he turned and gave her a quizzical look. They were standing right by the main door to the outside, and Meg could feel the cold blasting in every time someone left the school.

"Hey, how was Burger King yesterday?" she asked him.

His quizzical look turned to a scowl. "What's it to you?"

They weren't best friends, but he didn't usually treat her this way. "Just wondered. I heard you were there, hanging out with some babe from the big city."

"Who told you that?"

"My step-dad, Rich." She didn't feel like saying, my step-dad to be.

"I hate this place. Why don't people mind their own business?"

"What's the prob? I heard you were hanging with Danielle Walker. She's going to college, isn't she?"

"Hey, we just ran into each other there. No big deal. I kinda know her from this last summer. Met her at the beach. Then I did some work for her folks when they were at the cabin."

"Fine. Don't have to get so weirded out about it."

Curt came walking up. "Hey, guys. What do you say? Want to go sledding this aft?"

Meg loved to sled and Curt knew it, but she wished he hadn't invited Andy to come with them. Him being along would change the whole nature of the sport. She could just see those two guys, ramming into each other on the hill, having to make it into some big competition.

"Later, man," Andy high-fived him. "I got things to do."

Curt turned to Meg. "What'd you think?"

"It's pretty cold."

"Bundle up. Then when we hit a bump, you'll bounce."

"You two be careful. Sledding's not for sissies." Andy shook his head. "On the news they're saying that a lot of people are busting up their spines this winter because the ground's so hard and frozen. Who'd think sledding could be dangerous?" With that, Andy walked outside to catch his bus.

Curt slung his arm over Meg's shoulder. "I've got the car. Can I give you a lift home?"

"Absolutely. I'll even make you some hot chocolate." They dove into their parkas and scarves. "Did you know that Andy was seeing Danielle Walker?"

Curt popped his head through his hood and shook it. "Who's Danielle again? The name sounds familiar."

"You know that guy whose house you can see from Bogus Road. They're weekenders. She's his daughter."

"Oh, I think I know who you mean—that Danielle from the Cities. I remember seeing her around this summer. You're kidding."

"I can't believe you didn't know, what with you two being soul brothers and all, or is it comrades in arms?" Meg said.

"Never said a word to me."

"Hmm. Wonder why not. Doesn't seem like Andy." They linked arms and pushed out through the main doors.

"Oh, the guy can be deep."

"So deep that he didn't even tell you about her? I wonder what the big secret is."

CHAPTER 16

4 January: 4:30 pm

I thought *I* was going to stay with you for awhile at the cabin. I was planning on it," Danielle said, pouting as only she could do, while still looking fairly attractive at the same time.

Dan wasn't happy to see his daughter lodged in the doorway. She looked like she hadn't changed clothes in a few days and she had only a smear of lipstick on, not her usual full makeup. The set of her jaw and her stance told him she was upset.

He, on the other hand, was feeling pretty good, considering. He was glad to be back in real clothes and sitting up on the bed. But he wasn't looking forward to this conversation with his daughter, knowing how much she disliked Sherri.

"No, Danielle. That won't be necessary. Sherri and I have decided to give it another try. My accident has changed the way I'm looking at everything. I guess I'm seeing things more clearly."

She flounced into the room and stood in front of him, arms folded over her chest, blond hair falling around her face. "Oh, really? What's that about? I thought you two were through. That's what you told me. You said Sherri was just using you. That she was boring. What's with you?"

"Maybe I changed my mind. Maybe I know now that she's steady, not boring. Maybe I was wrong."

"Geez, Dad, for once you can admit it. That you were wrong about something. Big whooppety. Well, I think you're going to regret letting her back into your life. I don't want to hear about your problems with her anymore. As far as I'm concerned, she's a bitch. She ripped up my life when she took you away from mom."

"Danielle, give Sherri a break. You don't have to like her, but I ask you to be at least civil to her."

"Whatever."

He reached out for her hand, but she pulled away from him.

"Dad, you said you would give me some money. You promised. I need it now. You know, for the down payment on that condo I was looking at. Remember? You promised."

"Danielle, now's not the time. Wait until I'm feeling better. Besides, nobody buys a piece of real estate in the winter."

"What about you? You bought that stinking old farm. Stole it from an old lady, that's what you said. You bragged about it."

"Danielle, I'm your father. You need to calm down. That's different. I know what I'm doing. Listen, in a couple months I'll go condo shopping with you. We'll find you the perfect place."

"But this is the one I want. It's got everything—right by the lakes, workout room in the basement. Great view."

"Don't worry. Another one will come along just as good— probably even better."

Sherri picked that moment to walk into his hospital room and Danielle exploded. "I know this is all your doing," she yelled at Sherri. "You have always tried to turn my dad against me. If it weren't for you, I'd have my condo. You think you can step back into his life and take over again. Now he won't have any time for me. Like last time when you got married."

Sherri stared at Danielle and backed up. "What are you talking about?"

Dan yelled. "Stop it, Danielle. Now I mean it."

Danielle turned back toward her father and shouted, "I hate you. You're nothing but a big slob and a liar and a cheat. You cheat on everyone. Even me, your daughter. When you're lonesome you want me around, but now that Sherri's come back, you don't care about me anymore."

"Danielle, I'm just helping your dad out—" Sherri said, but Danielle broke in before she could finish.

"No, don't try to explain. I know the routine. He'll suck you back in until he sees some other piece of ass that he likes better. He did that with my mom. You think you're different. Yeah, you got him to marry you, but he's never going to really change."

Sherri pulled away as if she'd been slapped.

Danielle turned back to her father. "I never want to see you again." She stormed out of the room, then turned back and screamed. "So fuck you. You're not my father. I disown you."

Sherri sank down in the chair and stared at Dan. "What was that all about?"

"I'm sorry, Sherri. I'm not sure. She doesn't mean it. I just wouldn't give her some money." Dan wondered if that was all that was going on. "She's tired and worn down from being here. She doesn't handle stress well."

"Well, you've trained her. I think she equates your money with your love."

Dan was surprised to hear Sherri be so blunt with him. Maybe she had changed too. "You might be right. But she'll be back," Dan said, hoping it was true.

Sherri reached down and put a hand on his shoulder. She didn't look her best, but she was smiling. "Let's go home," she said.

4:40 pm

The Hegstrom house was hidden deep in the snow and woods. Claire went down many small roads, then a lane and finally turned into a long driveway that skirted a field and ended up in front of the house. A Christmas tree was stuck into a snowbank on the side of the drive with pieces of suet and other treats for the birds. She knew her way because she had been here once before to pick up some milk.

There was no path to the front door, but the steps to the side door had been shoveled. She walked up to the kitchen door and knocked.

"Come on in," she heard a voice yell from the interior.

Pushing the door open, she felt the steam from the kitchen hit her face. The smell of gingerbread wafted toward her as she closed the door behind her, hitting it with her backside to make sure it was tightly closed.

Sara Hegstrom walked into the kitchen and stopped when she saw Claire. "I wasn't expecting to see you." Claire figured Sara was about the same age as she was—mid-forties. She was a handsome woman with long tawny brown hair streaked with silver. She wore it tied loosely at the nape of her neck. She had on what looked like a hand-knit burgundy sweater and sweat pants with polar fleece booties on her feet.

"I need to talk to you and your husband about something. How's your daughter and the baby?"

Sara smiled and looked much more rested than she had at the hospital. "Much better, thank you. She's finally named him—Eric. Such a nice Scandinavian name. They're home and doing fine. Both of them are sleeping right now." Sara offered Claire a chair. "Should I get Clyde?"

"I think that would be a good idea."

She went into another room. Claire could hear the TV go off and moments later they were both back in the kitchen.

"To what do we owe this honor?" Clyde said rather boister-ously. He, too, seemed more relaxed in his flannel-lined denim shirt and jeans.

"I talked to your daughter yesterday."

They both sat down and a look passed between them. Clyde said cautiously, "Yes?"

"She told me who Eric's father is. Or rather I guessed who it might be and she confirmed it."

Clyde put his head in his hands. Sara shook her head leaned into him. "I don't know what to say. Clyde just told me. I could-n't believe it."

"Well, what happened between your daughter and Mr. Walker is against the law. Bonnie is a minor and even though it sounds like the sex was consensual she was under age. I want to know how you want to handle this."

"What are our choices?" Clyde asked.

"You could take him to court. When the minor is over six-teen years of age, as you daughter is, such and offense is con-sidered a class A mismeanor. It carries a maximum sentence of a fine of $10,000, nine months in jail, or both. Given how much older Mr. Walker is than Bonnie, he would probably be fined, I would guess might even serve some time. You could also prove paternity and he would be forced to help out financially with the baby."

The couple sat still.

Claire said, "Bonnie said she told you the morning of the birth who the father was. She said you were very upset when you learned how she had gotten pregnant, Mr. Hegstrom. How do you feel now?"

"You gotta understand," Clyde's nostrils flared slightly and his shoulders rose, a combative posture. "I went downstairs and my daugher had delivered a baby and was hemorrhaging in her bed. When she told me who had done that to her, I wanted to wring his neck. I just wanted to throttle him. But now that she and the baby are fine, I don't know what I want to do."

Sara lifted her head. "Whatever's best for the baby and Bonnie. We don't want them hurt. Do we need to decide anything right now?"

"No, but I would advise you to come to some kind of decision fairly soon. I think it will be better for all involved. The other thing that counts against him is that technically he was her employer—which might raise the stakes. He was in a position of power over her."

"I don't know what to say. He's always treated us well. He even gives me a holiday bonus, more than most of my clients around here do. I hate to lose that job, but I don't know if I could stand to see him again."

"By the way, Mr. Walker has admitted to having sex with your daughter, but he claims he thought she was eighteen."

"What the hell difference does that make?" Clyde stood up so fast his chair went flying backwards. "You would have thought we could have trusted him with our daughter. What kind of scumbag sleeps with a girl nearly young enough to be his grand-daughter?"

Danielle was getting into her car when she felt a tap on her shoulder. She turned and was not that surprised to see Andy standing there. He had called her three times on her cellphone, but she had ignored him. He did not like to be ignored.

"Hey," he said.

She almost thought of getting in and slamming the car door in his face, but decided it might be time to cut things off cleanly between them. She didn't know why he was bugging her now. They really hadn't had that much of a thing going. He just wasn't that interesting.

But she motioned him around to the side of the car. She might as well get it over with. Andy sank into the seat next to her. His face was red and he had a snowboarding hat pulled down over his forehead. He smiled and she thought once again what a cute smile he had, mischievous and naïve at the same time.

"Let me get the car going." She turned on the car and started the heat.

"What's going on with your dad? He leaving the hospital today? You going to stay with him?"

"Andy, this isn't working out, you and me. Besides, I'm getting ready to leave," she told him.

"Leave? What do you mean? Aren't you staying with your dad?"

"No, looks like he and Sherri might be getting back together. Which really fucks everything up. He doesn't want me to get the condo now." She shook her head. "Listen. I gotta go. Nothing is working out."

"Things could change," he said.

"I don't know. Things have changed. Like I said, he and Sherri seem to have gotten real tight again. It doesn't look like I'm going to get the money."

His face tightened. "I can't believe Sherri would go back to him after all that's happened. Where does that put you?"

Danielle was exhausted and didn't want to be sitting in a car in Durand, Wisconsin, talking to a punk kid about her dad and his bitchy wife. She wanted to get back to her apartment and sleep in her own bed tonight. "I guess that puts me out in the cold."

CHAPTER 17

4 January: 7 pm

How would you feel if some old guy had sex with Meg?" Claire asked Rich as they finished the lamb stew he had made. They were having a rare dinner alone. Meg had gone to study with a friend.

Rich frowned as he pushed back his plate. Her question had come out of the blue. "Where are you going with this, Claire?"

"Don't worry. Nothing has happened to Meg." She stood up and started to clear the dishes. That was their arrangement. He made the meals and she cleaned up after them.

"So what are you asking me?"

"Well, you know technically if Meg and Curt were to have sex now, which I'm not convinced hasn't happened already, it would be statutory rape. After all, he's eighteen and she's only seventeen."

"That's stupid." He laughed. "I mean, don't get me wrong. I'm not saying they should have sex, but it shouldn't be illegal."

"Yeah, I know, but that's the law. We do have discretion as to when to prosecute. Which brings me back to my original question—how would you feel if some old guy, you know, about your age, had sex with Meg? What would you do if you found out who the guy was?"

"So now I'm old." Rich leaned back in his chair. "That's easy. I'd want to pound the guy into the ground."

"Would you want to kill him?" Claire asked as she piled the dishes in the sink.

"Depends."

"On what?" She started to run some water into the sink to wash the dishes. There were so few of them she wasn't going to run the dishwasher, plus she liked washing dishes by hand once in a while.

"Oh, wait on the dishes. Come and sit down."

Claire wiped her hands on a kitchen towel and sat back down across from him. "Depends on what?"

"Well, I guess, primarily if it was consensual. On how Meg was doing with it all. How it happened. Many variables."

Claire said, "You are such a reasonable man. You want some coffee?"

"I wouldn't say no to a cup of decaf. Sounds good on this cold night."

Claire started the coffeemaker.

Rich watched her, then asked, "Is that what happened to Bonnie Hegstrom?"

She turned and looked at him. She was marrying one smart man. "You are capable of putting two and two together, aren't you?"

"Who was the guy?" Rich asked.

"Hey, you know I can't tell you that, not until it's public information. But I will say that it's no one you know well." She wanted to reassure him about that since he knew everyone.

"Hmm."

"But I'm trying to figure out what to do about it. I went and talked to her parents and they don't seem eager to prosecute. I know that Bonnie doesn't want to. She's said as much."

"But can't you just go ahead and do it?"

"Yes, we can. But it isn't usually a very good idea. Why waste everyone's time when the victim doesn't even want him to be punished?"

"I suppose."

"Bonnie's not dumb." Claire poured them both cups of dark brew. "But the thing I'm worried about is she needs to think seriously about getting some child support out of this whole mess."

"The guy got money?"

Claire looked over at him. "Rich, I've said all I'm going to say."

"Hey." He raised his hands up. "You were the one who brought it up. You ask my opinion and then you shut down on me. So here it is: Anyone who would take advantage of Bonnie Hegstrom, or any seventeen-year-old kid, should have the book thrown at them."

After taking a sip of the coffee, Claire said, "You know, what we're doing is technically illegal—living together and having sex without being married. The state of Wisconsin does not see us as moral, upstanding citizens."

Rich lifted his coffee cup in a salute to her. "Maybe we should break the law a few more times while we still have a chance?"

"Sounds good, but can we take a snow check? I'm utterly pooped. Something about this weather just makes me want to hibernate."

9 pm

"Well, if it isn't my little deputy?"

Amy had purposefully stopped by the Chippewa Tavern on the off chance that John Gordon might be there—she knew it was a hangout of his—and yet she was surprised when he came up behind her at the bar. She hadn't seen him when she walked in and there were only a handful of people in the place. Too dangerous to drink and drive in this weather.

John slid onto the stool next to her and smiled. His smile made his eyes crinkle until they almost disappeared. "Well, Amy, I hardly recognized you without your uniform and your hair down. What're you doing out on this cold night?"

"Same as you. Kicking back, having a brew."

"Let me get you that brew." He called the bartender over and then asked, "What're you drinking?"

"Whatever's on tap."

As he ordered she watched him. She couldn't believe she was having a drink with John Gordon. How things changed. When she was in grade school she used to watch him, the captain of the football team. She had a super major crush on him, but he was so out of her league. He was centuries older than her for one thing. And all the girls wanted to date him. If she remembered correctly he had been crowned homecoming king his senior year.

That was years ago. John was aging well. His shoulders still looked good under his sweater and there was no little pudgy potbelly forming that she could tell. From what she knew he wasn't much of a drinker. He didn't seem drunk tonight. But she was sure it got as lonely at his mother's house as it did in her apartment on these long winter nights.

He turned and handed her a mug of beer and then held his up and they clinked mugs. "How's Mr. Walker doing?"

"He's out of the hospital."

"I suppose he'll hightail it back to the Cities."

"No, don't think that's in the plans. He's going to stick around for a while until everything is more settled."

"Like what?"

"I can't talk about it."

He leaned in closer. "I like that—that you won't tell me what's going on with him. That's good."

"It's just the way we do things."

"You know at first I was surprised you became a cop. I thought you were more of the school teacher type, but since I've seen you in action, it suits you. I can see you take your job real seriously."

Amy had had about enough bullshit from him. "Stop talking to me like I'm one of your sister's little friends. I wouldn't have made a good teacher. Don't think I like kids that much, plus the thought of having to be cooped up all day long makes me antsy. With this job I get to move around, work on different cases. It does suit me."

He held up his hands to fend off her barrage of words. "Hey, I didn't mean to condescend. I was pretty serious about all that."

"You're not going to get me to talk about Daniel Walker."

"I'm not going to ask another question."

"Okay then." Amy decided it was time to quiz him. "So how are things going with your farm? What'd the lawyer tell you?"

"Nothing good." He ducked his head. "I don't want to talk about it."

"Then what should we talk about?"

"How about telling me if you're seeing anyone right now?"

"Not that I know of."

"What does that mean?"

"Why're you asking?"

"I'm going to stick around after all. I just don't feel comfortable leaving my mom the way she is. She's gotten a little nutty. So anyway, I thought maybe we could go out for a bite to eat some night or a movie."

"Are you asking me out on a date?"

"I guess so."

"I'm not too young for you?"

"As long as I'm not too old for you. What with me being old enough to be your father."

"You'd have had to start pretty young to be my father, like when you were ten."

John laughed and said, "I can't remember that far back."

"Sounds good."

They played a few sets of pool and each had another beer. Then they both noticed that, even though it was not even eleven yet, the bar had emptied out and the bartender was looking ready to leave himself, counting out the cash from the register.

"I guess it's time to go," Amy reached for her jacket.

John took it from her and helped her put it on. As he did he leaned in and kissed her on the neck.

Amy wanted more. She didn't want her night with John Gordon to end.

"I'm not sure you should drive home." She turned in his arms, stood on tiptoe and and kissed him quickly on the mouth.

When they pulled apart, he said, "Oh, really?"

"Yeah, I'm not sure how much you've had to drink, but if you tried to drive I might have to arrest you."

"Well, now, that would be mighty embarrassing. What're we going to do about this situation? You have any ideas?" He wrapped an arm around her neck and pulled her close.

"I don't live too far from here."

The deep kiss he gave her warmed her body in a way she hadn't felt since the hottest day last summer.

11 pm

From the way he was sitting—shoulders hunched, head lowered—Sherri could tell Dan wasn't feeling very good. He tried to act as if he was okay, but she knew he was tired. She was sure he hurt all over. The frostbite on his face had to be bothering him, not to mention his foot.

Before they left the hospital, the doctor had prescribed him some kind of pain pill. Dan said it helped some, but he needed to add some liquor to the mix. Of course, he wasn't supposed to drink with it, but he was working on his second large snifter of Courvoisier. No one could tell big, strong Daniel Walker what to do. She had given up trying. But sitting in her favorite chair next to him Sherri knew this was where she wanted to be. If only he meant half the things he had said recently.

The gas fireplace was on high. Sherri was always surprised by how much heat it gave off. She had wanted a real fireplace, but, as Dan had explained to her, a gas fire was more convenient and supposedly even more environmentally correct, but she missed the smell of wood burning in an open hearth.

Dan leaned forward and put his hand on her knee. "I got something to tell you, Sherri, and you're not going to like it."

"Thanks for warning me." She closed her eyes. She didn't want to hear him tell her that he still wanted to get the divorce. "I'm not assuming anything. I'm here because you need someone to take care of you."

"No, it's not about that. I was serious when I said I wanted to give it another try. I do think almost dying has made me a better man. Even as bullheaded as I am." He sighed and took another large swallow of brandy. "But it's confession time. Much as I hate to confess."

"Do we really have to do this right now?"

"Well, I know you're going to find out sooner or later and I'd just as soon the news came from me."

She was pretty sure she knew where this was going and she really didn't want to hear it. What did it matter who he slept with while they were separated? As long as it wasn't anyone she was related to or one of her best friends. "What did you do and with whom?"

"With whom? That's one thing I've always liked about you, Sherri darling, you speak such good English."

"You're stalling."

He put his head in his hands and looked down at the floor. "Did you know that Bonnie Hegstrom had a baby?"

"Bonnie? Our cleaning lady's daughter?" Even as she tried to sound nonchalant, her stomach was sinking. She felt a horrible tug in the pit of her guts. "She had a baby? But she's just a kid."

"Well, it might be mine."

Dan lifted his head up and looked at her. His eyes were flat brown like a piece of wood. He looked even worse than he had in the hospital and she wondered if the doctors had been right to let him come to the cabin.

Sherri could feel she was still resisting taking in what he was saying to her. She didn't want to know it. Shaking her head, she asked, "What are you saying? You slept with that girl?"

"And I really fucked up this time. I might get into a real legal mess," he said. "Bonnie's underage."

A knock sounded on the door. Two sharp raps.

"Who could that be?" Sherri asked.

"The cops might be here to take me away," Dan said with a slight laugh. "Or probably Danielle ready to make up with her old dad."

Dan stood up and hobbled toward the door. She should have gotten up and answered it, but she couldn't move. Danielle was the last person she wanted to see at that moment.

Sherri sat still in her favorite chair. But nothing seemed favorite any more. Who was this man she was married to? How could he have slept with Bonnie Hegstrom? What was love and sex and all of it to him? She realized she didn't understand him at all and wasn't sure she wanted to.

Sherri turned and watched Dan pull open the door. A wave of cold air poured in, sharp as teeth.

At the same instant, she heard a loud crack and saw him bend double. A tree breaking in half. Thunder crashing down on the roof. An explosion in a quarry, blowing rocks apart.

Dan fell in the entryway and the door banged shut in front of him. Her husband lay in a heap, a pile of flesh and bones. Nothing more.

Sherri stood up. Inside of her she was pushing this all away. This moment. This time when the world tore apart in front of her. She still held her snifter and could smell the deep sweetness of the brandy. The warmth from the fake fire made her sweat and shake at the same time.

She had to walk over to him.

It felt the same as when she found him in the snow. She knew he was no longer in his body. She knew that loud sound had been made by a metal object slamming all that made him human into oblivion.

Somehow she was sure this time her husband Daniel Walker would not be coming back from the dead.

CHAPTER 18

4 January: 11:15 pm

You told me to call…" A voice so shrill and hysterical came over the phone line that Claire had to hold the receiver away from her ear. Some woman was screaming at her in the middle of the night.

"Calm down. Who is this?"

Instead of calming down, the woman got worse, not even talking in words, but completely incoherent. The sound of her voice grew muffled as if the phone had been dropped, and then Claire could hear someone sobbing.

Keeping the phone receiver pressed to her ear, Claire stood up and moved away from the bed. Rich didn't need to be woken up too. She pushed her feet into her polar fleece slippers and grabbed her robe from the bedpost. Once out of the bedroom, she shut the door behind her.

"Hello?" she hollered. "Are you there?"

"I'm sorry," the voice said, then a loud jagged breath. "This time he's dead. He's really dead."

"Who is this?" Claire asked.

"Sherri Walker."

Claire's heart sank. This was not good. She had given Sherri her cell phone number when they were leaving the hospital, told her to call if Dan could remember anything new.

Even though Claire was sure she knew the answer, she had to ask, "Sherri, who's dead?"

"You know." The woman was crying again, but more quietly. "Dan. I can't stand it."

"Where are you?"

"At our cabin."

"What happened?"

"Someone shot him right in the chest. They knocked at the door and then they shot him."

"Who?"

"I don't know. I didn't see. Dan went to the door and opened it. Then there was a loud noise and he fell. I checked him and he's not breathing. I felt for a pulse, I did everything. He's gone."

"I'll be right there."

11:00 pm

As soon as they walked into Amy's apartment, John pushed her against the door and surrounded her. His arms held her against the door, his mouth pressed onto hers. He seemed ravenous, like he wanted to eat her up. His hunger made her realize she was starving too.

They started pulling off each other's clothes—scarves, mittens, coats, boots. When John lifted her sweater over her head at the same time that she was trying to undo his belt they fell onto the floor, cushioned by all their outerwear. He finished pulling the sweater off, turned to her, and started to laugh.

Amy looked at him and cracked up too. His hair was lifting off his head from static electricity. His shirt was half off. Then they kissed while laughing, but the laughter slowed them down and their love-making turned playful.

The first time took place on the pile of clothes after John pulled a condom out of his wallet. "Hope it's not too old. It's been in there for quite a while."

It was fast and awkward. Somehow in all their thrashing around Amy found herself halfway under the coffee table when they were done.

She held his head on her chest and said, "Would you like to try out the bed?"

"Bed sounds good. This floor's a little hard. I think I abraded my knees."

She grabbed his shirt. He pulled on his jeans, stood and walked around, inspecting her apartment. "This is cozy."

"Oh, I know it's small."

"Yeah, but it feels real comfortable."

Amy was proud of her apartment, the first place she had lived on her own. The small flat was above the pharmacy, only three rooms—a bathroom, bedroom, and then the main room which served as kitchen, living room and dining room.

"Let me give you the grand tour." She pointed out the new two-seater couch that she had bought at IKEA two months ago. "Very green. Made from all recycled material. The only new piece of furniture I own."

"The kitchen." She had cleared the dinner dishes off the counter, but they were still in the sink. The seventies décor looked awfully faded in the dim light.

"Very efficient," he said.

She walked down the short hallway. "The bathroom." This was the room she was most proud of. It had cool blue and white tile and she had bought new shower curtains to match. After painting the walls a gleaming glossy white, it looked crisp and sanitary.

"Convenient."

"And the bedroom." Amy had made this room her refuge. The bed was a queen with a white down comforter on it. Over her bed she had hung an old hooked rug of an owl that her grandmother had made.

"Very nocturnal," he said. "Nice."

Amy was glad that she had dressed her bed before she left for work that morning and that she had put on clean flannel sheets.

They moved slow, exploring. John kissed her in places no one had ever kissed her before: the palm of her hand, the crook of her knee. Slowly he opened her up until she felt like she had never been so vulnerable. When he entered her, it felt like he belonged there, inside her. They came together in a slow wave.

"Wow!" he said when he finally rolled off of her.

"Really?" Amy said, pleased.

"Wasn't it wow for you?"

"Triple wow."

"Then why really?"

"I don't know. I'm having a hard time believing this is happening. You know, with the homecoming king and all."

He leaned over her, his face so close she could hardly focus her eyes on it. "Get used to it, my little queen. It's going to be a long winter and I plan on keeping you warm."

Amy was not used to hearing such sweet words from a man. Bill had been fun in a blustery sort of way. A good guy, but pushy. Plus, she had always thought of John as brusque. To find this warmth hidden under all that gruffness was so surprising.

Amy was in the bathroom, washing herself, when the phone rang. She had left it on the bedside table. John picked the phone up and brought it to her. She read the screen before connecting.

"Shit! It's work. I gotta take this." She answered, "Hello?"

"Amy, I'm sorry to wake you, but Daniel Walker's been killed. Over at his house. I need you to call the Crime Bureau and then get your butt over there. I'm just leaving my house now. I'll meet you there."

"Okay," Amy said and clicked off. She closed her eyes, wishing she didn't have to say what she had to say. "I gotta go."

"Now?"

"Yeah, someone killed Dan Walker."

"You're shitting me?"

"Nope, I'm not." She stood up and kissed him. "All I can say is you've got a damn good alibi."

11:25 pm

Without waiting until the car warmed up, Claire pulled onto the highway barely able to see. Her breath was freezing to the inside of the car window so Claire tucked her head into her jacket collar. The defroster wasn't making a dent in the frost and she could only see through a small hole in the windshield. Thank god it was the middle of the night and no one was out on the roads. She was going about thirty miles an hour down Highway 35.

Claire hated to think what she was going to find when she got to the Walker's. When she had worked in Minneapolis, there had been a homicide nearly every day. Down in Pepin County, years passed with no one getting killed. Sheriff Talbert teased her that murders had gotten much more frequent since she had come to work for the department. Before her joining the force there hadn't been a murder in the county in almost twenty years. Then Claire's neighbor Landers Anderson had been killed. That was ten years ago. Since then they had averaged nearly a homicide a year. Claire blamed it on the influx of "foreigners," which in Pepin County meant anyone from outside the county, like her.

A shooting like this needed to be handled carefully. She would find a bloody body waiting for her, a hysterical wife, a crime scene that needed securing in this blasted cold weather. She hoped the crime lab would get there soon. She already knew she would want tire mark prints and footprints. If they hadn't drifted over.

As Claire turned up the hill away from the lake, the darkness deepened, the bare branches of the trees folding in over the road. The cold landscape entered her body. Winter was beautiful down in the coulees, but brutal. Even though heat was finally coming out of the blowers, Claire shivered compulsively, in hard jerks.

It wasn't just from the cold.

Sherri's voice had reminded her of her own hysteria nearly ten years ago, when her husband had been killed. She remembered the moments after Steve had been killed so vividly; they were tattooed into her psyche.

He had been hit by a truck on the road right in front of their house. Meg, eight at the time, had seen it happen, then hidden in the curtains. Claire remembered starting to scream. The calm, effective Minneapolis homicide detective couldn't stop shrieking as she tried to bring her husband back to life, as he was dying in front of her. She couldn't remember when she gave up, when she finally stopped. The sound of her screaming she still heard, sometimes in a dream, sometimes seeping into her waking life.

After a near nervous meltdown, Claire had left the cities so she would never have to experience that kind of evil again. Every year she had lived in the country she felt herself melt and unwind from what she had been put through, felt herself begin to trust the security and warmth she got from Rich, the safety in this small and tight community, where people watched out for each other.

She didn't want to have to see another woman's anguish that might so clearly mirror what her own had been. As she got close to the driveway turn-off, she slowed down even more.

In order to not ruin any marks—footprints or tire prints— Claire decided she better park out by the road and walk in alongside the driveway. The turn to the Walker's driveway appeared in her headlights and she pulled over and sat for a moment. The stars shone brittle in an infinitely dark sky. No warmth from those solitary wanderers, no solace anywhere.

Claire pulled in closer to the side of the road, blocking the end of the driveway so that no one could make the mistake of driving down it. She pulled her hat down tight on her head and, bracing for the cold, got out of the car.

Her shoulders automatically constricted, pulled in as the cold air hit her. She could feel her lungs constricting, protecting themselves. The air was so frigid it hurt to breathe. Again, Claire tucked her face into her jacket collar. She walked along the road and then waded into the snow alongside the plowed path of the driveway.

When Claire got close to the house, the light by the front door illuminated her way. She watched where she put her feet, not wanting to obliterate any recent prints. She was able to make it up the front steps and get to the front door by stepping only in unadulterated snow.

When she pulled open the door, she saw Sherri sitting on the entryway floor with her husband's head in her lap. The woman was bent over and her hair was covering his face. Soft sounds were coming out of her mouth, but Claire couldn't tell if she was gently weeping or praying or talking to her husband.

"Sherri," Claire said quietly, not wanting to startle her. "I'm here."

As if he were still alive and could feel what she was doing, Sherri stood up and gently placed Walker's head on the floor.

Claire kneeled down, needing to check to make sure he was dead. She could see the small hole that had been blown open in his chest, near or next to his heart, a splat of blood surrounded it. As soon as she put her fingers on his neck, she could tell Daniel Walker was dead. Already heat had fled his body, leaving it plasticy and lifeless. No breath, no pulse. Dead.

Sherri was swaying back and forth, saying, "No, no, no," her arms wrapped around her waist as if holding in her guts.

A resonance hummed in Claire, a huge desire to join this woman in her weeping and anguish, but she fought it hard, swallowing it down her throat as if it were a piece of food she could not longer chew.

Claire stood up and put her arms around the shaking woman. Then she pulled Sherri in tight, trying to hold her together. The wailing sound in her ears tore at her.

"You're okay. It's going to be okay," Claire said, even though she knew she was lying.

CHAPTER 19

5 January: 8:45 am

A punk weapon," Jed Bartholomew said, rolling a small shell casing around in his gloved hand. "Usually used for squirrel hunting and even then you have to be pretty handy. I tell you it's really a fluke this guy died from it. Either the shooter was just plain lucky or a hell of a shot."

"Or both," Claire said. "This isn't going to help us locate the killer given how common a shotgun is."

"Yup, you can say that again," Jed said smacking his lips together. An arms specialist from the crime bureau, he was within moments of retirement. Claire had been surprised and very happy to see him arrive at the scene. As far as she was concerned, he was one of the best in his field. "I'd be surprised if there isn't one of those shotguns in just about every farmhouse from here to Durand. Not worth much either. So whoever used it will probably just dump it. No great loss."

"You're a bundle of optimism this morning."

"Morning?" Jed looked out the back of the house. "So it is."

As he talked, Claire had been watching the first glow of the sun tinge the snow on the horizon. It would still be another hour or so before the sun crested the land, but it was already lighter out.

"The wife seems pretty distressed." He spoke more softly, even though they had finally persuaded Sherri to retire to the bedroom. "You don't think she had anything to do with this?"

"Doesn't look like it. From what I can see of the marks in the driveway and the position of the body, it happened the way she said it did. I think, even though they had had their problems, she loved him. Plus, she's a city gal. I'd be surprised if she knows how to shoot a gun." Claire felt a tug at her heart, remembering Sherri's sobbing. "But, you know, she was there. Her husband was killed right in front of her eyes. That can get to you."

"You did a good job at this crime scene, routing everyone in through the bottom door, cordoning off the whole driveway," he said as he bagged the bullet casing and marked it.

"Thanks. I didn't want anyone to plow into the tire marks. Yeah, now if that blasted print examiner would just get here."

"Don't be in such a hurry. Nothing's going to melt in this cold. Plus, you need to have pictures taken before he gets to work."

"As soon as the sun's up, that's going to happen. Jerry's been working on it but he's having problems with the camera freezing up."

Jed slapped his hands together. "Nothing like doing an outdoor crime scene in below zero weather, is there?"

Claire stared at the spot where the sun would emerge from the land. Any minute now. She desperately needed more coffee.

8:50 am

"If in doubt, shoot it," Amy told Jerry after he had asked her what she wanted photos of. "You know Claire, she goes for overkill. We won't have a second chance with these prints."

"Freaking cold." Jerry asked, "Have they made more coffee? I'm freezing out here."

"You're not alone. Get those tire tracks over by the snow-bank and I think that's it. Unless you see any others."

As she watched him set up for the last few photo shots, she stomped her feet and thought of John, probably still sleeping in her bed. They had stayed up awful late. What she wouldn't give to be lying next to him.

Besides being cold, there was another reason Amy couldn't wait for Jerry to finish. She wanted to watch Ted Lawson, the print examiner, take the castings of the tires and foot prints. She had heard he was one of the best in the field. The longer she worked in law enforcement, the more interested she was in the forensics aspects. She was even seriously considering going back to school to get a degree.

When Jerry finished, they both went in the house to warm up. Someone had raided the kitchen and made some coffee. Black and gritty, just the way she liked it. A shot of pure caffeine would keep her on her feet for a few more hours.

Amy found Lawson out in the garage, setting up buckets and other equipment. "How're you doing out here?"

The tall, thin man wiped his hands on his insulated pants. "I think I've got what we need. We really lucked out with this garage being heated. I wasn't looking forward to working out-side today, but this will definitely make it easier."

"If you don't mind, I'd like to help you."

"Seriously. You want to be out there in that weather?"

"I've never seen this done before in snow. Is it much harder?"

"There's an extra step, but I've got the special wax we use for this, so it shouldn't be too hard." He added, "I'd love some help.

Let's mix the dental stone in here. First we'll go out and set up the forms. You know which ones you want prints of?"

"I think so, but you can tell me what you think. I've got them marked with flags."

"It's going to take a while. The wax needs to set up for a few minutes before we can pour the cast."

They both bundled up, covering every inch of skin, and went back outside. Over the next few hours, Amy helped him set forms around each print, spray the wax over the impression, and then mix dental stone using very cold water. Then they'd cover the impression with a box and let it dry while they started to work on the next one. When they had impressions of all four wheels and multiples of each shoe, they decided they had enough.

Amy's fingers were numb and she was shaking with exhaustion, but thrilled that she got to work with Lawson. She was drinking more coffee and standing next to him, looking over their work. The castings covered the floor of the garage in rows, reverse images of the prints in snow.

Lawson said, "Nobody thinks to cover their feet. Wouldn't be that hard. Just slip on rubbers or booties or something. We would still be able to tell a few things, like their approximate weight, but that wouldn't give us much evidence. Sure they wear gloves and put masks over their faces, but then they tromp all over, leaving tracks that are easy to find, especially in snow. Lots of info in foot prints."

"It's almost all we've got on this guy." Amy asked, "What can you tell from these prints? Anything jump out at you?"

"So this is what we know: the guy—I'm assuming it was a guy since most women don't wear a size 12—was wearing some kind of boot, I'm guessing either a Red Wing or a Timberline. Hard to tell without studying them. They make a very similar impression. I'm also thinking he wasn't overweight. The prints weren't too deep. The boots look fairly new, there's not a lot of wear on them." Ted stared down at the prints that were lined up in the garage. "All I can say is if you find the guy and find his boots, you've got him. These are nice clean prints."

"What about the vehicle?"

"I'm not as good with tires. Not my area of expertise, but those are good tire prints. Again, crisp and clean. Looks like some kind of truck. Notice how wide apart the wheels are. But those tires are worn. So I'd say some kind of old clunker."

"Thanks for letting me help."

Ted lifted his coffee cup. "Any time. You do good work."

Amy found Claire sitting at the kitchen counter and filled her in on what Ted had told her.

Claire wrote a few notes down, then said, "Listen, go get a couple hours of sleep and then I want you to drive into the Cities and find Danielle and let her know what's happened to her dad. I know it's an hour and a half drive, but I'd rather you tell her in person. Sherri said she went back to the cities today. You've got her address in town, don't you?"

"Yeah, I got it at the hospital."

"I want you to drive up there and talk to her in person. I want you to see how she reacts. I doubt she's involved, but I want to check out everyone that's on our list of suspects. We know she doesn't drive a truck. However, I need to go talk to Clyde Hegstrom and then I'll drop in on John Gordon. A guy who wears boots and drives a truck—could be either one of them."

"About John Gordon…" Amy started. Like pulling a bandage off skin, do it quick.

Claire must have heard something in her voice, because she lifted her head up and looked at Amy. "Yes?"

Amy faced her square on. "He wasn't wearing boots last night. I know because his shoes are under my bed."

9 am

The sun glared doubly in her eyes, once through the pale blue sky and then again off the glazed snow crust. There was a crystalline quality to the landscape, and Claire felt like it was cutting her up into little pieces. She felt tired, not just from waking up after only a few hours of sleep, but tired from seeing what people did to each other. As she drove out to the Hegstrom farm, she realized she didn't want to have to ask these people what they had been doing last night. She knew it was her job, but suddenly it seemed immensely rude.

Then there was Amy.

Just when she was thinking how far along Amy was coming, she'd gone and done something so stupid as to sleep with a suspect. Claire could already hear the sheriff reaming them both out. One of the hazards of working in a small county. Everyone knew everyone and even occasionally slept with them.

As Claire turned down Hegstrom Lane, she gave herself a pep talk. Do your job, do it well. One step in front of another. The one thing she was sure of was she wanted to find who had killed Daniel Walker. She wanted Sherri to have some kind of closure—more than she had had.

When she knocked on the door, a female voice said, "Come on in. It's open. I have my hands full."

Claire pushed through the door and stepped into the warmth of the kitchen. Bonnie Hegstrom was sitting in rocking chair in the corner of the room with her baby in her arms, her tawny hair streaming down her shoulders. Claire quietly walked forward. When she got close she could see that the baby was sleeping. His eyelids were like pale pink shells with threads of purple, quivering. His full lips were slitted open, a bit of baby spit on his chin. He looked so peaceful. A calmness emanated from them both.

"Finally he's sleeping," Bonnie whispered. "He was up all night."

"Sorry to hear that."

"Mom says it serves me right. I guess I didn't sleep through the night until I was two. Or so she's claiming."

"Where are your parents?"

"Mom's downstairs doing wash. We're really going through the diapers. And Dad's sleeping. But you don't need to talk to them. We all discussed the situation and we're in agreement. We don't want to press charges against Mr. Walker."

"What about child support?" Claire blurted.

"We'd like to handle that privately."

Claire was so impressed with how adult Bonnie had become, not that she had known the girl much before. But from how Meg had described her, Bonnie had sounded like a quiet girl. Maybe having the baby would give her some self-assurance.

As if reading her thoughts, Bonnie said, "I never would have thought having a baby would have been a good thing, especially

right now. But I'm actually glad. I wake up and he's there staring at me, and I feel happy. I want to take care of him. I want
to finish school and go to college and get a good job so I can
take care of him. I've never felt like this before."

Funny what love can do to a person, Claire thought. "That's
great."

"Anyways, that's what we decided about Mr. Walker."

"Well, I might need to talk to your dad."

"I hate to wake him. He had a pretty rough night."

"How so?"

"Well, he got up with the baby after midnight and didn't get
back to sleep for an hour or two. We're kinda taking it in shifts.
I'm not sure how long my parents'll last, but I feel like I'm getting my strength back already."

Relief flooded Claire. This was the best kind of absolute
alibi, being unasked for made it that much stronger. "So your
dad was here all evening?"

"Oh, yeah. Too cold to go out for anything. We just sat in
front of the fire and watched Eric." Bonnie rubbed her baby's
forehead with one finger. "I can't believe how I never get tired
of him."

"There will be times."

"Oh, I'm sure. But right now, he's perfect."

"Hey, Claire. Cold enough for you?" Sara came into the
kitchen with a basket of diapers on her hip and set it down at
Bonnie's feet. "Might as well fold them now, Bonnie. Nice to
work with them while they're warm. Slip the baby down into
you lap and you should be able to manage them. I know it's asking too much of you to put him down for a second."

"Mom, you know he wakes up if I put him down."

"He's got to get used to it. Especially if you're planning on going back to school soon."

"But he's so little."

Sara beamed down at her grandson. "Wouldn't know it from the caterwauling he did last night." Then she asked Bonnie, "Did you tell her our decision?"

"I did."

Claire cleared her throat. "Well, I have some news for you two. I just came from the Walker's. Daniel Walker was killed last night." She hesitated about saying how it had been done.

"What happened?" Sara asked.

Bonnie's eyes filled with tears. "Killed? But he didn't even get to see Eric. His son."

"I can't say much more. We're still looking into it, but I wanted to come over and tell you myself."

Sara straightened her shoulders and stated, "Clyde was here all night long. None of us left the house."

"I know. Bonnie made that clear."

"I'm so sorry for his wife." Sara bowed her head. "That poor woman. Was she there? Is she all right?"

"She's not hurt, but she's devastated, as you can imagine. Losing your husband twice in a couple days would do anyone in."

CHAPTER 20

"Something bad happened last night," Meg told Curt as they sat next to each other in the lunchroom.

He handed her one of his peanut butter cookies and she gave him half of her apple. "What? How do you know?"

"Mom tore out of the house in the middle of the night. I woke up but was too tired to look at my alarm clock, but it was pitch black out. I don't think Rich even woke up. He didn't know anything about it when I got up this morning. But I heard her go. When I left for school this morning, she still wasn't back. So I assume it had to be pretty bad."

"What's that like? Knowing your mom is going to some weird, gory scene?"

Meg thought for a second. "I worry sometimes. Not so much down here, but when we lived in town, that was scarier. She really doesn't talk about her work much. In fact, when it's the worst is when she gets really quiet. She just goes away."

"My mom gets like that. Dad says it's her time of life. But I like the quiet better than the bitch-o-rama."

"Yeah, I know what you mean." Meg looked around the lunch room. "Where's your bud, Danger Man?"

"Don't know. He didn't show up today. He's been threatening to take his own private snow day."

"I like that. I can't believe I actually like an Andy idea." Meg regretted what she said as soon as the words left her mouth. Since Curt had accused her of being jealous, she was working really hard on not being so negative about Andy.

"Well if I know Andy, a snow day has little to do with snow. He's probably been playing GTA for a million hours." Curt rubbed his forehead. "I don't know how he can keep at it for as long as he does. Or, who knows, maybe he's hanging with that Danielle."

Meg had been shocked when she heard that Andy had been seeing Danielle Walker. She remembered seeing her once this fall at an event at the Lake Pepin Art Center, when they had brought in a film and the director. Danielle had been there, wearing boots that came up above her knees. And they had looked good on her. Not only was Danielle a few years older than Andy, but she seemed really snooty, like she would have thought she was way too cool for a kid like Andy. "I don't know which is worse."

"I think you might be right about one thing."

"Only one thing?" Meg teased him.

"I'm starting to think too much of those video games can really warpify your mind. I'm even playing the games in my dreams. It's like I can't get away from them." He grabbed hold of his head and shook it. "He does like to ice fish. Maybe he's out there staring into that freezing water."

Meg was so relieved to hear Curt talking about what was going on with Andy and how so much video-gaming was affecting him. Maybe she would get the old Curt back again. "I suppose you could take a break from the gaming."

"Yeah, I guess. It's just hard. I want to play. It's like a compulsion." He pretended like he was armed with a game, air-playing. "Plus, it's winter and there isn't a lot else to do."

"Why don't you come over later?" She didn't want to push him too hard, just make a suggestion. "We could play chess."

"You mean like on a board?" He bumped her with his shoulder.

"Yeah, do you remember how to move little figures around with your hands in real reality?"

He burst out laughing. "Real reality. Good one, Megsly. I guess I could try to remember how to play chess, for you."

"Well, remember this—I beat you last time." She poked him in the ribs.

Curt stuck his chest out and thumped it. "I am King of the chessboard."

"But in chess the King has little power. It's much better to be Queen."

3 pm

When Danielle opened the door, Amy was struck by the fact that they were about the same age. For some reason she hadn't really remarked on that before. Maybe it was because everything else about them was so different.

Not only that, but seeing Danielle in her home environment, Amy saw how truly gorgeous she was. In the hospital, she had looked wilted, with her hair tied back in a ponytail. She was wearing her hair down and it hung below her shoulders in a heavy honey-brown hue. She had enough make-up on to enhance all her already-perfect features, but not so much that it drew attention to itself. She was wearing a soft blue cashmere sweater—at least it looked like what Amy thought cashmere would look like—over a pair of wool pants.

All this made Amy feel more geeky than usual. The department uniform was not exactly the most stylish. The regulation pants had never fit her well. She had hips where it had none, which made the pockets flare out in a really dorky way.

"Danielle? I'm Amy—from the Pepin County Sheriff's department." Amy was nervous about giving Danielle the news and she could hear her voice was shaking.

Danielle tilted her head to the side and crinkled her nose. "I know you. You were at the hospital." Then her voice rose as she asked, "Why are you here?"

"Yes, well, it's about your dad." Amy remembered Claire's advice about giving relatives the bad news. Do it quick. Don't make them wait. She launched in to her practiced line. "I'm sorry to have to tell you that your father is dead." Amy stopped there. Let that news sink in before she went on with more specific details.

Danielle backed up into her apartment. "Dead?" Her voice wavered and she sounded younger. "But I thought he was doing okay. The doctor said he could go home. Sherri was going to take care of him. What happened?"

"He was shot. When he opened the front door."

"How could he be shot? What front door? At home?" Danielle sat down in a chair in the entryway and folded in on herself, her head in her hands. After a moment, she righted herself, flung her hair back, and asked, "Goddamn it. Do you know who did it?"

Amy could see that Danielle was fighting tears. "We're not sure yet. Working on it."

"When did it happen? Was it Sherri?" Danielle stood up. "I don't trust her at all. She's been taking my dad for a ride this whole time."

"We're just not sure."

Danielle motioned Amy into the apartment. Amy pointed down at her boots and Danielle said, "Don't worry. The cleaning lady is coming tomorrow."

A large black leather couch was covered with old antique-looking throw pillows. The view from her fourth floor apartment was of downtown Minneapolis. The place, like Danielle herself, looked expensive and perfect. Comparing it to Amy's own apartment was like comparing her outfit to Danielle's: ordinary and practical to extraordinary and excessive. Amy wondered what her place would look like if she had a lot of money.

Wiping at her eyes, Danielle asked, "You came all the way up here to tell me this?"

"Yes, well, we knew how hard this would be on you. It's not news we like to deliver over the phone."

Danielle looked around as if there was something she should do. "Can I get you something?"

"I'd love a cup of coffee."

Danielle turned toward the kitchen, which was galley style with a pass-through to the living room. "I hardly ever make coffee here. There's a Starbucks just down the block. But I think I might have some."

Amy didn't think she wanted to watch this process, plus wasn't convinced the end product would be any good. "A Coke would be fine. Anything with caffeine."

"I have a Red Bull."

"I'll try it."

"Don't you have those in Durand?" Danielle pulled a can out of the refrigerator and handed it to her.

"I'm sure we do." Amy followed her into the living room where Danielle arranged herself on the couch. Amy sat in a modern looking swivel chair that was as uncomfortable as it looked. She was afraid if she leaned back in it, the whole thing would tip over.

"So what happened?" Danielle asked.

Amy told her as much as they knew. As she did tears ran down Danielle's face, smearing her eye make-up.

Danielle reached into the pocket of her pants and pulled out a wadded Kleenex, loudly blowing her nose on it. For some reason, this homely action made Amy like her better. "What did you mean you thought this would happen?"

"Well, geez, someone already tried to kill him once. I've thought all along that it was Sherri. I know that everyone thinks I'm a bitch to her and she's this great nice woman who puts up with my father, but that isn't exactly the way it is. She stole my dad away from my mom. You can't believe the things she did."

"Like what?"

"She called our house and told my mom that my dad was with her. Otherwise, I'm not sure my mom would have ever figured it out. I had a suspicion. I knew that he was taking more business trips than usual. Mom tried to ignore those kind of clues. She just didn't want to know. So there was a big scene about the other woman. But by this time it was really my mom that was the other woman. Sherri was in charge. My dad did anything she wanted. She really knew how to work him.

"As soon as they got married, she started milking him. A new car, new clothes, new house. I know my dad isn't always easy to live with, but Sherri pushed him pretty hard too. Then when he finally got tired of her, he's like the bad guy for wanting something more."

"So you think she might have killed him to get his money? But I thought that you said he had changed his will?"

"Yeah, he told me he did. But who knows. Plus, she's still married to him. It would be awful easy for her to contest the will and if I know Sherri that's exactly what she'll do."

Amy took a sip of the pop. A pack of Smarties is what it tasted like. "Well, at the moment, it doesn't look like she did it. Do you know if your father had a gun in the house?"

"Not to my knowledge. He was never a hunter. Didn't really like the woods at all. A golf course was what he thought all of nature should be." Danielle thought for a second, then asked, "So where was Sherri when it happened?"

"She was in the house. Her car was in the garage. The tire tracks don't match either car."

"Oh." Danielle's eyes turned down and she tapped her lip with a long fingernail. "Was he shot with a shotgun?"

"Yeah, how did you guess that?" Amy asked, wondering how this city girl even knew what a shotgun was.

Danielle's face went pale and blank. "It might be my fault."

4 pm

"Rich said you wanted to be woken up now."

Claire opened her eyes to see Meg standing over her. The world swam into focus. She pushed herself up in bed and realized she hadn't even taken her uniform off. But that was probably a good thing. Then she wouldn't have to get dressed again. She glanced out the window. There was still some daylight. She would have time to go back to the department and check in with everyone.

"I brought you a cup of coffee," Meg said, handing it to her.

"You're a doll." Claire took a deep sip of coffee, blessing both her daughter and her about-to-be husband. If she wasn't marrying him anyway, she'd marry him for his coffee.

"What happened last night? Rich said someone got killed." Meg sat down on the edge of the bed.

Claire knew the news would be blasted all over the papers tomorrow: Daniel Walker was a prominent member of Twin Cities society. "You know that guy who almost froze to death?"

"Mr. Walker?"

"Well, he was killed last night."

"Like murdered killed?"

"I'm afraid so."

"That's Danielle's dad, right?"

"Yes, why?"

"That's weird. Curt and I were just talking about her at school today. How strange it is that she's going out with Andy Palmquist—you know that friend of Curt's. The one I told you about who's so into violent videogames. Calls himself Danger Man. Curt said he's getting kinda weird."

"Hmm."

Claire's cell phone buzzed on the nightstand. When she answered it, she heard Amy's voice saying something, then breaking up. "What?"

"I'm on my way back, but I wanted to tell you..." The phone cut out for a second, then Amy was back on.

"I didn't get that. Repeat it."

"Danielle thinks Andy Palmquist might have had something to do with Walker's death."

"Andy?"

Meg looked at her.

"I'll check it out." When Claire hung up the phone, she asked Meg, "Was Andy at school today?"

Meg shook her head. "What's going on?"

"I don't like coincidences."

CHAPTER 20
5 January: 4:30

In the middle of the winter, the sun set way too early. Claire turned the car lights on as she drove down highway 35. The last traces of the sun were fading from the south-western sky, straight across the lake. Claire knew there would be no moon tonight. Since she had moved down to the country, she paid attention to the moon cycles like some people watched their stocks. She knew tonight was a new moon, which meant nothing showed in the sky. If you looked hard you might find a black orb, but that was all.

As she was driving down Hegstrom Lane, she knew she was coming close to the Palmquist's driveway when a pickup truck shot past her. She saw that there was a single man in the vehicle but in the waning light couldn't make out more than that.

She parked out front of the house and walked up to the side door. When she knocked a thin woman wearing a green and gold sweatshirt came to the door, looked Claire up and down and then asked, "What can I do for you?"

Claire was surprised by how young the woman was and asked, "Are you Mrs. Palmquist?"

"Yes," the woman said a little defiantly. She crossed her arms and stood halfway out of the door.

"I'm Claire Watkins. I work for the sheriff. I was wondering if your son Andy is here?"

The woman couldn't be more than late thirties. She must have had Andy when she was still a teen. "Nope. Just left."

"Do you know where he went?"

"Didn't say anything to me. I'd guess he might be going hunting since he had his shotgun."

Claire didn't like this at all. Too late in the season to hunt, and too late in the day. "Kinda late to go hunting?"

"Sometimes he shoots squirrel."

"You know where he might have gone?"

"Why'd you want to know?"

"I just need to ask him a few questions."

"He in trouble?"

"Not necessarily. Was he here last night?"

"Far as I know."

Claire decided not to push it. Her main objective right now was to get to Andy before he could get rid of the gun, if that's what he was up to. Why wouldn't he have dumped it the night before? She needed to find out. "He driving a red pickup?"

"That's the one."

Damn, Claire thought as she climbed back into the squad car. I should have followed my gut and turned around when I saw the truck leaving. She turned back toward the lake and punched the accelerator. The squad car squealed and slid, then careened down the iced over road as the speedometer hit fifty.

4:35 pm

When Rich walked in the house it was so quiet he thought no one was home. He sloughed off his coat and unwound his scarf, then looked into the living room. Meg and Curt were sitting across the table from each other, staring at something. Took him a second to realize they were playing chess.

"Hey, you two. What's up?"

"I've nearly got his queen," Meg bragged.

"Don't get your hopes up. My knight has plans for that little lady."

"Where's your mom?" Rich asked. "She get up?"

"Yeah, I woke her like you told me. She went off to talk to Andy Palmquist. He might be the killer," Meg announced.

"Meg, don't say that. You don't know," Curt said. He glared at her. She glared back.

"When did she leave?"

"About a half hour ago, I'd guess. Maybe not so long. How long have we been playing, Curt?"

"Close to that."

"She said to tell you she'd be back for supper."

"I was thinking about making some chili."

"And grilled cheese?" Meg added.

"Sure. Curt, you going to join us?" Rich asked.

"Sounds good."

4:40 pm

"Thanks for driving me," Danielle said in a quiet voice, "I'm not sure I could have done it."

"No problem." Amy was glad to hear her talk. Danielle hadn't said anything since Prescott, about fifteen miles ago. She was starting to get worried about her, wondering if she was going into shock or something. For that reason, Amy had turned the heat in the squad car on full blast.

"I don't think I could have driven right now. I can't feel anything, like this isn't real." Danielle slapped her hands together.

Amy was glad she knew the curving path of Highway 35 as well as she did because it was pitch black outside. Her headlights shone on the snow-packed sides of the road. "How'd you meet Andy?" she asked.

"Down at the beach last summer. Nothing else to do in that stupid little town so when I went down for the weekend with my dad, I figured I might as well work on my tan."

"Isn't he kinda young for you?"

"A couple years. He was fun. Again there's not a lot of choice down there. Most of the guys who hang out at the bars are gross. At least Andy wasn't gross. Plus, he has a good bod." Danielle continued, "I don't want you to get the wrong idea. We only hung out a couple times. It wasn't that serious or anything. What's really weird is that he came up for a picnic one day and kinda got along with my dad. And Sherri thought he was darling. I don't really get it."

"Why do you think he might have killed your dad?"

"It's just that he got so mad when he heard about my dad not giving me any money for my condo. I don't know. I think Andy thought that if I could get the condo then I'd be in his debt or something. It sounds crazy, but I just think he did it."

CHAPTER 21

5 January: 4:40 pm

Claire caught up with Andy's truck as he drove across Highway 35 going toward the lake.

She hated to think about what might have happened to her car if she had skidded off the road as she took the turns around snow-covered fields too fast. But she had caught up to him. He was about a block ahead of her. She slowed, hoping he might not notice her.

He passed Main Street and drove down the hill to the lake, then bumped over the railroad tracks and went off the road and headed to the beach on a snow-packed road made by various vehicles going out on the ice.

She stopped at the top of the hill and watched the pickup truck start out across the lake. In the distance she could see the night-time glimmerings of Lake City in Minnesota; closer in, the dark shapes of the ice-house village past the middle of Lake Pepin. That appeared to be where Andy was headed.

An ice house.

Not a bad place to dump a gun. No way to get to it before spring and by that time it could have been carried halfway to New Orleans. The boy wasn't stupid. She turned off her headlights and drove slowly down the hill. She wanted to get as close as she could before he saw her coming. If he went into an ice house, she might be able to get the jump on him.

As the squad car crunched across the frothy ice at the shoreline, she saw him drive into the jumble of shacks. She hung back as he parked the truck and then sped up slightly to get in closer. When she was within a few car lengths, she turned off the car and let it creep forward with leftover momentum. She tried to call for back-up but her phone wasn't connecting. She'd have to chance it.

Andy entered an ice house. Claire jumped out of the squad car and ran after him. Running on the snow-covered ice was not easy and she needed to keep her eyes on the ice house so she wouldn't lose track of which one it was.

The cold tore at her throat and lungs, wind whipping up chunks of ice off the ground-up snow. Her feet slid as she ran and once she went down on one knee but pushed off and ran up to the ice house.

Claire stopped for a second to catch her breath and figure out her best strategy. He had a gun. She couldn't just burst in on him. Even if he had done nothing wrong, he was liable to shoot at her.

Darkness gathered around the edges of the lake, with the ice glowing phosphorus white as if lit from underneath.

The sound of a gunshot tore out from the ice house, echoing out and out across the lake.

4:50 pm

"Where do you want to go?" Amy asked as they drove through Maiden Rock. The little town was deserted, only the Christmas lights dangling from the light posts gave any sense that there was life in the town.

"Do you think I can see my dad?"

Amy knew the body had been taken to the morgue. "Now? I don't think so. Do you really want to?"

Danielle shook her head. Then she said with a trembling voice, "I don't know. I feel like if I could, it would help me believe what is happening. Do you think you could get me in to see him? Like I could identify him. They do that all the time on TV. They always get to see the body."

"Not tonight. Maybe we can set it up tomorrow. Where do you want to go tonight?"

"I don't want to stay in that stupid motel again. That was horrible. I suppose up to the cabin."

Amy couldn't stop the snort that came out of her, but was instantly sorry. "Just doesn't seem like a cabin."

"That's what my dad called it. His cabin. He loved that place. He really did. I know you think he was just a rich bastard, but he loved me." Danielle started to cry. "I can't believe he's dead."

"I'm sorry." Amy said as she turned up Rustic Road leading to the top of the bluff. The effects of almost no sleep were starting to come crashing down on her. She wanted to get rid of Danielle and get home to her bed before she plowed off the road and ended up in a snowbank.

When they arrived at the Walker's "cabin," all the lights were on, as if that would keep away the dangers. Danielle got out of the car and stood looking at the front of the house.

When Sherri opened the door, the warm air of the house billowed out, foggy and visible.

"What do you want?" Sherri asked. "I thought the cops were done here."

Amy felt compassion for both of them. When someone was killed there was so much anger and no place to put it. She could feel the tension between the two women and hated to think of them lashing out at each other. Neither of them needed or deserved that. She stepped in. "I brought her down, Mrs. Walker. We needed to question her. It would be great if you could put her up for the night."

Danielle flashed her a look of relief. Sherri grudgingly held the door open for both of them.

Danielle walked in and put her small tote bag on the floor of the entryway. "I'm sorry about Dad, Sherri."

"Yeah, it's been awful."

Danielle folded in on herself, her arms crossing over her stomach. For a moment, she said nothing, then she looked up at Sherri. "And it might be all my fault. I didn't realize Andy was going off the deep end. I think I might have pushed him too hard. I'm afraid that he might have killed Dad."

Sherri rocked back in horror. "Andy? Not Andy? Why would you think that he might do it?"

4:50 pm

The silence after the gunshot was immense.

Claire listened at the door of the icehouse, then heard an odd sound, like someone was scratching at the ice. What had happened in there?

After unholstering her gun, she grabbed the door and pulled it open, standing to the side of the entrance. A light illuminated the interior of the ice house and she could see inside and what she saw pulled her forward.

Andy had his back to her and was kicking at a hole in the ice, working at making it larger. He held the shotgun in his hand while he kicked at the hole with his heel. He had blasted a hole in the ice with the shotgun, but it was not big enough to push the gun through it.

When the door swung back, he turned and saw her, then tried to jam the gun down into the hole.

Claire moved forward and grabbed the butt of the gun. Andy let go and stepped back. Suddenly he was behind her. She was thrown off balance and he pushed her, sending her stumbling toward the hole. Both guns went flying as she fell.

At the same time that her head hit, she felt her right leg plunge through the ice, the tight hole scraping her pants as her leg submerged. The water was beyond cold, it was searingly frigid. She had to get her leg out. She clawed at the hole, trying to release her leg. Pushing herself up on one knee, she managed to pull free.

Behind her the door slammed shut. Andy had left and taken both guns with him.

Her head reeled and she fell down onto the ice and blacked out.

CHAPTER 22

5 January: 6:15 pm

I can smell the chili," Meg said, walking into the kitchen. "How spicy did you make it?"

"Just a mild blow-your-head-off. I thought you said your mom would be back soon," Rich said, stirring the chili.

"You know her. I told you she was just going over to the Palmquists to ask Andy some questions. But you know how she gets when she's working on an investigation." Meg threw her arms up in the air. "Time loses all meaning."

Curt walked in behind Meg and draped his arms around her shoulders. She snuggled back into him.

Rich loved seeing these two together, so easy and natural with each other. However, he wasn't sure he wanted them to be together forever. He hated the thought of neither one of them exploring love with anyone else, but how nice to meet someone at such a young age to learn from.

"Well, she's been gone way over an hour. I think I'll try to raise her." Rich called her cell, but it went right to voice mail. Then he called the sheriff's department. Susan, the new office manager, told him that she hadn't heard a peep from Claire. When he asked for Amy, she told him that Amy had checked in a few minutes ago and said she was headed home.

Andy Palmquist lived just outside of Pepin, which was less than ten minutes away. If she was going to do something official—like arrest him—she would have called the sheriff's department. At least that's the way she usually did it.

"Let's give her another ten minutes. If she doesn't show, we'll eat." He didn't like that Claire had been gone so long on what was supposed to be a casual conversation, but he didn't want to let Meg know how worried he was getting.

Maybe it was the cold that was making him more nervous than usual about her being late. What if she had slid off the road? What if she was stranded someplace? In this kind of weather, a few minutes could make a huge difference in survival.

6:15 pm

When Claire came to, she was shaking so hard her teeth were chattering. She knew this was not a good sign. Her leg felt like it didn't belong to her anymore. She had to get to her car. Sitting up, her head ached, but she didn't feel like she would pass out again. Move slowly, she told herself.

When she tried the door to the icehouse, she found she was locked inside. She was so cold she was having a hard time focusing her mind. All she could think about was the absence of heat, how all-enveloping it was.

She went to the far side of the structure away from the door and forced herself to run at it. The space was small, only about a couple yards, and she had to watch out for the hole. She slammed her shoulder into the door and felt it give. Something was starting to wrench free. Maybe the hinge on the door.

She lunged at it again and this time heard a crack. She could see it was shredding where the door met the lock.

One more time she stepped across the small space and threw her full force at it, body slammed it. The door ripped apart and she fell as it splintered open. At least the snow softened her fall. Near total darkness outside, but by the faint ambient light she could make out the darker shape of her squad car.

Picking herself up she limped over to the vehicle. Her frozen leg was nearly useless. She had no feeling at all in it and her wet pant leg had hardened into an ice cast. The door to the squad car was open, but when she looked inside, she couldn't see the keys. She slid into the seat and looked under the seat.

No keys.

Andy must have grabbed them.

No matter. She could get help.

She picked up the radio to call in to the office for help, but then found that the wires had been ripped out.

Panic started to fill her up. She had to get someplace warm. Her leg was leaving her.

6:45 pm

After dinner, Rich put the cover on the chili and left the pot on the stove. Claire could reheat it when she got home.

The chili hadn't tasted as good as he had hoped, lacking in something. Or maybe it was just him. Maybe he was the problem. He couldn't help being mad at Claire for making him worry again. He had to learn to let go of that. She had proven to him time and time again that she knew what she was doing.

Susan called from the sheriff's department. "Hey, Rich. Has Claire shown up yet?"

"No, she's still not back."

"I just tried to get hold of her on her car phone and it wouldn't go through. Something's not right. Do you know where she is?"

Rich felt a sheet of ice water run down his back. "Meg said she went to talk to Andy Palmquist. Do you want me to call over there?"

"Why don't you? Get back to me. I'll keep checking around."

Rich called the Palmquists. When he asked to speak with Andy, Mrs. Palmquist was quite abrupt, saying simply, "He's not here. Don't know when he'll be back. Maybe he's down to his house," and hung up.

Meg and Curt had come into the kitchen and were watching him.

"Andy's not there. His mom said something about his house. What does that mean?"

Curt twisted up his face, then said, "I think I know. Andy has an ice house out on the lake."

"Let's go," Meg said.

"Not you," Rich said. "Someone needs to stay here in case she calls. Curt can come with me and show me where the ice house is."

"You're not leaving me behind. I'll go nuts."

Rich looked at her. He knew it would be harder on Meg to stay behind that almost anything that might happen if she was with him. "You can come if you promise to stay in the truck."

The three of them pulled on their boots, down coats, hats and mittens and were out the door, climbing into Rich's pickup.

"Go down to the Pepin Beach," Curt said. "His ice house is straight out from there."

They were quiet on the way over, but as they bumped down to the shoreline, Meg said, almost to herself, "Mom is careful. Super careful. Something's probably just funky with her car phone."

Rich nodded and started out onto the ice. The rutted road was easy to follow across the lake, the indentations holding his wheels in place. When they got to the edge of the icehouses, all looked quiet. No lights, no sounds. Then he spotted the car.

"There's a squad car," Curt said at the same moment.

"What the hell is going on?" Rich asked as he scrambled out of the truck. The two teenagers followed suit.

The door to the squad car was hanging open and the interior light was still on. When Rich looked inside to check the phone, he could see that the wires had been pulled to it.

"Man, I do not like this."

Meg let a sound between a squeal and a whimper. "Where is she?"

Then she whipped around, cupped her hands to her mouth and screamed as loud as she could, "Mom!"

And again, "Mom!"

They listened to the call bouncing across the lake and hitting the bluffs on either side.

CHAPTER 23

7:00 pm

Claire sat down for a moment to rest. Her leg didn't feel so bad anymore. Just a gentle throb. Her face felt warm. She took off her hat. She knew she needed to get home, but she was getting so tired.

She had lost the car tracks and was trying to figure out which way to go. The icy snow made it hard to walk. The hard crust on top would break and she would fall through and then have to pull her legs out. Her frozen leg made walking difficult anyway.

She would take just a short rest. She could see the lights of town. It wasn't that far away. After a minute she would get up and start walking again. But now she felt like taking a break.

Claire lay back in the snow and looked up at the stars. So cold and puny. She blew out a stream of breath and it reminded her of the smoke from a cigarette. She remembered doing that as a kid at the bus stop, pretending she was smoking.

Just as she was feeling herself drift away, she heard Meg calling her.

What was her daughter doing out here? Shouldn't she be home in bed?

Claire sat up and looked around.

Again, her daughter's voice came across the lake, "Mom!"

Claire knew that Meg would keep calling until she answered. That kid never let up. She yelled, "Over here."

7 pm

Heading back to Durand, Amy was so ready for sleep that she could taste her bed and smell how sleep would roll over her. She had gone home in the morning for a rest and was disappointed to find that John had already left. His car had been parked only a few blocks away at the bar. But she could smell him on the sheets.

When Amy crossed the city limits, she called in to the department and Susan told her that Claire had gone missing and that the last known place she had been was the Palmquists.

Without another word, Amy turned her squad car around and headed back to Pepin, knowing she wouldn't sleep if she didn't know that Claire was okay. On her way, she called Claire's house, but there was no answer. She wondered where Rich and Meg were on such a cold night. She hoped not out looking for Claire.

For some reason, Amy wasn't that worried about Claire. She had never known her to get into trouble. It was probably the weather that had caused her phone to go out. This severe cold made everything harder. But Amy did want to follow up on it.

Amy let her thoughts drift back to John. She saw him as she had left him, drowsing in bed. How she would love to find him there again, waiting for her. She was still so surprised by what had happened between them. While she had been attracted to him, he was not what she would call the man of her dreams. He was not even her type, if she had such a thing.

She usually went for the louder, boisterous kind of guy—like Bill. Someone who was the life of the party, someone who could make her laugh. But with John she felt like she was on solid ground, literally that she knew where she stood. He had made no bones about the fact that he wanted her. She could tell he wasn't fooling around and that scared her and delighted her at the same time. Maybe she was growing up and was ready for a real relationship.

Tearing her mind away from thoughts of John, she looked for the turnoff to Palmquists'. If she remembered correctly, they lived past the cemetery off N, but close to town. She found the house easily and drove in behind a pickup truck. When she stopped, she felt like she was ready to lay her head down on the steering wheel and go to sleep. She didn't want to leave the warm cocoon of her car. But she forced herself out into the cold and walked up to the door.

Before she even knocked the door flew open and Mrs. Palmquist was talking to her. "It's Andy. He came home about fifteen minutes ago and went right out to the barn. I'm scared. He took his gun and he seemed like he was going to do something crazy. Please stop him."

"Call the sheriff," Amy said, then drew her weapon and walked to where the woman had pointed, to a pole barn behind the house. Lights were on in the building and she crept up to the door and nudged it open.

Andy stood in the middle of the space, his back to her, pretending to shoot his shotgun at some enemy that Amy couldn't see.

Amy had her gun at the ready. As he started to swing around to face her, she called his name. "Andy, put the gun down."

He lifted the gun up and fired into the air. The sound cracked the air like thunder. "No one can stop me. I am Danger Man."

In that moment, she saw him so clearly as a young boy, caught in a game that he didn't know how to play. "What're you going to do?" She knew to keep him talking. Hard to shoot a gun when you were talking.

"I'm in too deep," he said. "I just have to shoot my way out."

Whatever he had done, Amy was not going to contribute to his paranoia. Keep it simple and real. "Listen, your mom's scared you're going to hurt yourself. Put the gun down and let's go inside and talk." She took a step toward him. While she had her gun trained on him, he still had his pointed up in the air.

"Too late for talking," he said.

"Never too late for that. We can figure this out." Amy kept inching closer to him, hoping to get a chance to disarm him.

"I don't want to do this anymore." He let his shotgun fall toward the floor, one hand holding it.

"I don't blame you. Let's just call it a day and go inside and get warm."

He shook his head and suddenly seemed to see her. "There's no turning back." He started to lift the gun.

Suddenly Amy saw his intention. He wasn't lifting the shotgun toward her, but swinging it up to point at his own head.

His mother's voice called from the door of the pole barn, "Andy, don't."

Andy turned toward the voice and Amy bolted toward him and swung her gun arm as hard as she could. The weapons connected and the shotgun went flying out of Andy's hand. She grabbed his arm and forced her gun into the side of his neck.

He stood stock still and said, "Shoot me. That's what I want. Just shoot me."

"Come on, Andy. We need to talk." She started to move him toward his mother, who was still standing in the doorway. "Let's go back to the house."

He offered no resistance. His head down he walked toward the door. All he said was, "I did it for her."

9:30 pm

To rewarm her leg, as soon as they were home, Rich had put her in a lukewarm bath. While she complained of pain as feeling was coming back to her leg, none of the skin was waxy or yellow so he didn't think there had been any permanent damage. Her leg was red and swollen and blistered in a few spots, but Rich didn't think she needed to be taken into the hospital. After gently drying her off, he wrapped her leg in a loose bandage.

He managed to convince her to crawl into bed. He also got her to take a couple Tylenol. When Amy called and told them that she had taken Andy Palmquist into custody, Claire finally relaxed.

After Rich had turned off all the lights in the house, said good-night to Meg, who was reading, he walked quietly into their darkened bedroom and climbed into bed. He was surprised to find that Claire was still awake.

"You came after me," she whispered. "You found me. You always find me. If it weren't for you, I might be dead."

"Now don't go getting all mushy on me."

"No, I mean it," Claire said more clearly. "This is good. I've been figuring out something, Rich."

"What's that?"

"I think I know why I resisted getting married to you for so long."

"Really?"

"Yes, really. It has to do with my first husband." She nudged her head into the crook of his arm. He tightened his grip on her.

"Hmm."

"I think I was worried that if I married you, you would get killed, like he did, because of me. I didn't really know that's what I was thinking until I saw Daniel Walker dead, his wife holding his head in her lap. I remember how I felt when Steve was killed and I never wanted to go through that again, and somehow I thought, if I didn't marry you, then you wouldn't get killed. I could keep you safe."

"Makes a convoluted sense."

"Isn't that the only kind of sense there is?"

"I guess." He thought for a second, then asked, "But now you do want to marry me?"

"Yes, I think I'm finally trusting that you won't get killed. And you more than proved that tonight."

"How so?"

"Well, not only will you not get killed, but you'll save me." She started to cry.

"And you save me." He kissed her wet face. "Go to sleep. I'm right here."

CHAPTER 24
6 January: 9:15 am

For all his height, Andy Palmquist looked like a young boy when Claire walked in the conference room to talk to him. He was wearing the orange uniform of a prisoner and his eyes looked bruised as if he'd been crying all night long. She wouldn't wonder he had. How had he come to this? How could he possibly have killed a man? She was about to try to find out.

"Hey, Andy," she said as she pushed open the door. "Surprised to see me?"

He looked up, defensive. "I told that woman where you were. They told me you were all right," he said quietly, his head facing the table, his elbows holding him up on either side.

She waited to see if he'd say more. She had come to learn how effective silence could be in an interrogation.

"I'm sorry," he finally said. "I just didn't know what to do."

Claire turned and asked Amy to bring her a large coffee and a can of Coke. Then she walked in and sat down across from Andy. She had some papers that she shuffled around while she waited for him to lift his head.

Finally, he looked up again. "I don't know what more you want to know. I already said I did it, that I killed him."

"Yes, I know. Amy told me." She stacked the papers with a slap. "I just have a few questions and I was wondering if you could help me understand why."

"Just for fun, I guess."

Claire waited a beat. Then she tapped the table once with her pencil and said, "That's not what Amy said. She said, last night, you told her you did it for 'her'. Who's her?"

He shrugged.

Amy came to the door and handed her the drinks.

"You want a Coke?" Claire asked.

He shrugged again. She took that as a yes and pushed the can across the table to him.

"Andy, this is very serious. You're old enough that you could be charged as an adult. Unless you start talking, there's no way you're going to see the light of day again. We might be able to help you if we knew why you did this."

"I don't know," he mumbled. He put his hands around the Coke can but didn't open it.

She waited.

"He bugged me."

"How?"

"He thought he was so great. Like he got everything."

"So you killed him because he bugged you? That seems a little extreme."

"What do you know?"

"Not much," she conceded.

He lifted his eyes to her. "He pulled people in, promising them stuff, and then when he was tired of them, he'd push them away."

"Did he do that to you?"

"No," Andy said and looked down again. "I didn't really know him that good."

"Who did he do that to? Danielle?"

"Yeah, sometimes."

"You and Danielle were friends, weren't you?"

"Yeah, we hung out."

"Did you kill Mr. Walker to help out Danielle?"

He shook his head.

"Was he being mean to her?"

"Kinda?"

"Like what?"

"Just like that. He was a puppet master. Pulling the strings. Controlling everything."

"It's hard to watch that sort of thing, isn't it?"

Andy popped the Coke and took a swig. He nodded.

"What made you do it, Andy? What pushed you to shoot Daniel Walker?"

"It just got to me."

"What?"

He didn't say anything.

Claire decided to tell him what she had seen. "I was up there right after he died. Mrs. Walker was holding his head in her lap, tears streaming down her face. You killed her husband."

He lifted his head up at the mention of Sherri's name, then asked, "Sherri? She was crying?"

Claire noticed the surprise and anger that was in Andy's voice. A thought flashed through her mind. "Yes, she was crying. She was very upset."

"But she didn't love him. She told me that." His hands locked together as he struggled with this news.

"That's who you did it for, wasn't it, Andy?"

"He treated her like shit. Sleeping around on her. I just wanted her to be free of him."

"You did it for Sherri, didn't you?"

"She acted like she loved me. Then it changed. He wanted her back again. I couldn't stand the thought of her being with him, that old man."

"It wasn't Danielle," Claire said, more to herself than to Andy.

"Danielle and I went out a few times, then she brought me home to meet her parents. That's when I met Sherri. She had me come up to the house to help her with the garden. We got to know each other. I'd never met anyone like her. Then when they separated, I'd drive up to the cities to see her. She made me promise not to tell anyone what was going on between us until the divorce was final. But I know she loved me. I just wanted it to stay that way."

"What happened between you and Sherri to make you want to kill Mr. Walker?"

"As soon as he got hurt, it all changed. She wouldn't answer my phone calls when she was at the hospital. I knew she was there. I had to talk to Danielle to get any information on what was going on. Sherri totally cut me off. I couldn't stand it."

"So you went to their house. Did you intend on killing him?"

"Danielle told me that Sherri was there in the house with him. I couldn't stand it. She was supposed to be with me. I didn't want him to put his hands on her. She said it was over between them. I just wanted to stop him from touching her again."

12 February: 5 pm

"Even I was taken in by her," Claire said to Rich as she packed their suitcase for their brief honeymoon. He was sprawled on the bed watching her. "Sherri admitted to having a fling, as she called it, with Andy. She claimed she was just so hurt by Walker wanting a divorce and that Andy was right there. The more I think about it, the more I feel that Daniel and Sherri were really meant for each other—both of them fooling around with kids half their age."

"So Andy pled guilty?"

"Yes, thank god. For a while his lawyer was threatening to throw the blame on Sherri. I was not looking forward to having to go to trial with that case. Andy saw reason, I think his mom had a good talking with him, and he took the twenty years. For a kid that age that has to seem like eternity."

"I imagine."

"His mom brought in his gameboy and I swear he sits in his cell and plays it twenty hours a day."

"Stupid videogames. But I guess they're one way to avoid thinking about what's going to happen."

"I suppose." She folded his flannel pajamas and tucked them in next to hers. They were only going for two days so she was just packing one suitcase. "What's weird is that Daniel had actually cut Sherri out of the will so she won't be getting a cent from the estate."

"So Danielle gets everything?"

"No. It gets even better. Because it was written that the inheritors were to be his progeny—he didn't stipulate Danielle—Bonnie's little boy will be getting half the estate. That will go a long way to helping her out. She just got the results back of the DNA test which proved that he was Walker's son."

"Nice compensation for her," Rich said.

"I guess." Claire pushed down on the pile of clothes. She had a little more room in the suitcase. "You want me to pack another pair of jeans for you?"

"Why don't you throw in my corduroys, they're a little more big city."

"Red Wing's really the big city." Claire laughed.

Claire tucked in the pair he handed her and managed to close the suitcase. "The weird thing is that Andy swears up and down that he did not lock Daniel out of his house on New Year's Eve. He says he was at a party, which Meg and Curt confirm, and then he headed right into town to see Sherri. Which also gives Sherri a rock-solid alibi. Maybe Sherri was wrong about the door being locked." Claire scrunched up her shoulders. I guess we'll never know."

5:15 pm

As she drove up to the top of the bluff, Amy noticed a light shower of snow. The temperature was still sub-zero and it didn't usually snow when it was this cold, but this was a phenomena she had noticed all her life. Rather than the snow falling out of clouds in the sky, these flakes seemed to precipitate out of the brittle air.

She was nervous. Not that she was worried about meeting John's mother, because she had already met her many times, but more about how John would treat her in front of his mother. It was her first official visit to the farm as his girlfriend.

John and she had fallen into the habit of him coming over to her apartment when she was done with work two or three times a week. They would get a pizza or throw together some dinner—she was surprised to find that he wasn't a bad cook—and then just hang out watching TV or sometimes playing cards, 500 or gin rummy. Then he'd stay the night. She was a little worried about how close she was getting to him, not knowing if and when he would have to leave again for work.

But he had asked her to come to the farm for dinner and then said that if she wanted to she was welcome to stay overnight there. Amy had brought her flannel nightgown, but wasn't sure she would be comfortable spending the night. Even though they were grown adults, it would just seem weird to do that with his mother there. She'd have to see how she felt once she was there.

She turned in the well-plowed driveway. John had been picking up some money plowing out driveways for people and certainly did a nice job on his own. Amy could tell he was getting a little stir-crazy and she hoped that he would find some steady work soon.

When she entered the house, she relaxed. The kitchen was warm and bright, the table set with colorful fiestaware.

"We're having pork roast and potatoes. Nothing special. But I made an apple pie. How does that sound?" Edna Gordon asked.

"Sounds great. I haven't had a roast in a while. When you live alone, doesn't make sense to cook like that."

Edna nodded. "I know. When John was gone, I'd often just have a baked potato or scrambled eggs for dinner. That's no way to eat. I'm glad to have him back."

John came in with a bottle of wine. "I dug this out of our basement wine cellar. All three bottles down there. But one of them was this champagne." He held it aloft. "We're celebrating. I wanted to wait to tell you tonight, Amy. We have the farm back." He walked over and gave her a kiss on the lips.

"Wow! That's wonderful!" Amy's heart leaped. He would be staying on to work the farm. She was so relieved.

John popped the cork and Edna pulled out three dessert glasswares, explaining, "We don't have any of those special glasses for this bubbly. We'll have to use these."

"How did this come about?" Amy asked.

"Well, Danielle didn't want to go through with the purchase," John said. "I guess she's got her eye on a condo in the cities. She has no use for a farm. So she released us from the contract."

They all lifted their glasses. John said, "To the farm. May it stay in our family forever."

"I'll drink to that," said Edna.

They all clinked glasses.

The dinner went fine. The pot roast was well-cooked, probably overcooked, but it was just the way Amy liked it, with the meat crisped on the outside.

Finishing up the champagne with a slice of apple pie, she was full and happy. John had been very affectionate with her and Edna very welcoming.

"This was absolutely wonderful, Mrs. Gordon," Amy said after eating her last bite of pie.

"Heavens sake, call me Edna. If you're going to be staying overnight, you can't keep that up."

Amy looked over at John and he just smiled back at her and asked, "How was work today?"

"Well, we got the news that Andy Palmquist pled guilty to Daniel Walker's murder. He's looking at twenty years in prison."

"Poor boy. Not that he doesn't deserve it for killing Mr. Walker, but that man was no good," said Edna as she started to clear the table.

"But we still don't know how he got locked out of the house on New Year's Eve." Amy said.

Edna stopped what she was doing and said, "You know I've been wondering about that. I didn't think to mention it at the time."

"What, Mom?" John asked.

"Well, what really happened to him? I'm not really clear on that."

"Where have you been?" John said.

"I don't know. I haven't gone any place. It's just been too cold."

"Well, he was taking a sauna and went outside to cool off and somehow got locked out of his house. He almost died."

Edna sat back down in her chair. "Oh, no."

"Mom, what is it?"

"Well, I might have done it."

Amy couldn't believe what she was hearing. "What do you mean, Edna?"

Edna shook her head. "I went over to talk to him."

"What are you saying?" John asked.

"Well, you were so upset about the farm and it was all my fault. I thought I'd try to make it right. I couldn't get to sleep on

New Year's Eve and you had already gone to bed. I decided to take a ride on the snowmobile and see if I couldn't get him to change his mind."

"In the middle of the night?" Amy asked.

"I knew he stayed up late. I thought maybe he would be in a better frame of mind. I just didn't know what else to do. I had John's key to the house. They asked me to water the plants when they weren't there. I drove over and went in, but I couldn't find him. I knew he was there because I could see faint tire tracks, but no one was in the house. I figured he had gone out for the evening. So I just went around the house like I usually do and checked all the doors. The back door wasn't locked so I locked it."

"You didn't see him outside?"

"I wasn't looking for him outside. I did glance out the window, but it was too dark to see anything. Never thought another thing about it." Edna's face was drained of color. "I almost killed a man. How do you like that?"

CHAPTER 25

I do," Rich said.

Then Margaret Qualley, the only female Pepin County judge, turned to Claire and repeated, "Will you, Claire, take this man, Rich, to be your husband, your partner in this life, honoring him and loving him all your days on earth?"

Claire choked up. Rich held her eyes. She could feel hers filling with tears. She swallowed and said loudly and clearly, "I do."

"I now pronounce you husband and wife," the judge said, then added, "You may kiss each other."

Rich took her by the shoulders, pulled her to him as she wrapped her arms around his waist. They had a long and deliberate kiss. They had been practicing for this moment for years.

A cheer went up in the large auditorium above the Abode gallery. In the 1800s the space had been a theater, then in the early 1900s was turned into a gymnasium and was now a special events space for all sort of arts happenings. Claire had given in to Rich's wish that they invite the whole county so she wasn't even sure how many people were there. They were all standing in the midst of the tables circling the room with Claire, Rich and the pastor in the middle.

Since there was no aisle to walk down they simply turned and smiled at everyone.

Rich announced, "Let the party begin!"

On this cue, the DJ started the song from Hair, "Let the Sunshine in!" They were surrounded by well-wishers in a love-fest of hugging, kissing and crying. Dancing broke out around the room, grandmothers dancing with grandsons, even the Sheriff and his wife joined in. Claire noticed that Bill had brought a new date with him. Thank goodness Amy was happily dating John Gordon.

Rather than a sit-down dinner, Claire had insisted on a more party atmosphere with hors d'oeuvres circling the room, while local beers and Prosecco from the Palate were served from the bar.

She and Rich finally sat down at what was the head table, but in the round. Bridget sat next to her with her new beau, Satish. Her four-year-old daughter Rachel was tucked in between them. Meg and Curt had just pulled up two chairs next to them. Stewart and his long-time boyfriend Harry, sat on the other side of Rich and across the table was a very happy Amy holding hands with John Gordon.

Claire looked around the table and realized she was right where she wanted to be and so happy to be there.

Bridget leaned over and said, "Mom would have loved to have seen you in that dress."

"I can't believe you saved it all these years," Claire said as she ran her hands down a gown that her mother had bought for a cruise that she and their father had taken. From the seventies, the cocktail dress was nearly back in style, the top was off-the-shoulder in deep blue velvet with a knee-length gathered skirt made of heavy silk. Claire had taken the bow off the back and had it dry cleaned but other than hadn't needed to do anything to it.

All along she had insisted that she did not want to wear a traditional wedding dress, certainly not to wear white. "All I want is to be elegant and at the same time be able to dance."

Claire watched as Meg walked up behind Rich and draped herself over his shoulder. She knew her daughter was happy that they had married and Rich was planning on adopting Meg within the next couple months. "Then if he croaks, I get the farm," Meg had crowed on hearing the news.

"I can't see you staying on the farm," Rich had replied.

"It will be my retreat. I'll have my studio here."

Rich looked so handsome in his father's old sports coat and black wool pants with a white shirt and matching blue velvet bow tie. She didn't believe in matchy-matchy for couples, but this small touch pleased her.

All over the room a high tinkling sound started as people tapped their forks against their glasses.

Rich leaned toward her, she nuzzled into him, and they kissed for what would not be the last time that night.

And even though, outside the tall windows of the auditorium, it had just started to snow in what would come to be known as the Valentine's Day Blizzard, Claire felt safe and warm in a way she had never felt before.

Mary Logue is an award-winning poet and
mystery writer. She was born and raised in
Minnesota. Her most recent books are *Dop-
pelganger*, a middle-grade mystery she wrote
with Pete Hautman; *Point No Point,* her
ninth crime novel; and *Hand Work,* her fourth
book of poems. *Meticulous Attachment* was
awarded honorable mention by the Midwest
Booksellers Association in 2006 and *Dark
Coulee* won a Minnesota Book Award in
2000. She has also published a young adult
novel, *Dancing with an Alien.* Her non-
fiction books include a biography of her
grandmother, *Halfway Home.* She has been
an editor for several publishers. She is cur-
rently teaching at Hamline University in St.
Paul in their Children's Literature MFA and
lives with writer Pete Hautman and toy poo-
dles Rene and Jacques in Minnesota and
Wisconsin.